The Painted Alphabet
A mythical story of
Bali

The Painted Alphabet
A mythical story of
Bali

by

Diana Darling

EDITIONS DIDIER MILLET

Copyright © Diana Darling 1992

First published in 1992 by Houghton Mifflin

Published in 2011 by Editions Didier Millet Pte Ltd
52, Genting Lane #06-05
Ruby Land Complex 1
Singapore 349560

@ Second edition 2019, 2023

ISBN: 978-981-4610-79-7

Cover: Detail of a drawing by I Gusti Nyoman Lempad,
Siladri's wife falls ill (1950s; private collection)

Printed in Singapore

For all my teachers

Introduction (to the 2019 edition)

This little novel is loosely based on a very long Balinese poem called *Dukuh Siladri*. The story used to be performed in Bali in the 1930s as a play leading up to the ritual combat between two sacred effigies: the guardian dragon Barong and his nemesis, the terrifying Rangda. The outcome was always inconclusive, but often ended in violent trance, which foreigners like me adore. This was the ritual theatre that fascinated Antonin Artaud: a theatre of danger, or "cruelty" as he put it — "a spasm in which life is continually lacerated" — inspired by the performance of a Balinese troupe in Paris in 1931.

In the early 1980s, when I was still new to Bali, I was reading about Balinese ritual plays and discovered a synopsis of the Dukuh Siladri story. The only people I knew who had ever heard of it were elderly Balinese. Upon mention of the story, they would burst into song, singing the verse about when Mudita meets Kusuma Sari in the mountain forest of Gunung Kawi.

What intrigued me in the synopsis were the talking animals and the scene where a young witch has just finished bathing in the stream and has almost finished getting dressed. She sees a man coming and promptly gets undressed again.

These two elements made me long to see a revived performance of *Dukuh Siladri*. Together with John Darling, to whom I was married at the time, we commissioned an Arja performance (a form of Balinese opera) for a temple festival in the village where we were living, with the proviso that they perform this story. I imagined fascinating New York-style rehearsals and the preparation of special animal costumes.

To my surprise, the troupe didn't even discuss the performance until an hour beforehand, when the leader of the troupe outlined the story and assigned the roles. It was an Arja performance much like any other. So I decided to write the story as a novel, for my own entertainment. That way I could do whatever I wanted with it. The matter of cultural appropriation never occurred to me and was not an issue among the Balinese, for whom art was traditionally anonymous.

Over the next several years I casually collected oral versions of the story and blocked out its main structure. Later, after I'd started writing the book (in about 1987), I found a typewritten transcript of the poem, in Balinese language but Latin script, some 88 pages long. By now I had remarried and it was with the help of my second husband, Anak Agung Alit Ardi, that I read this. Agung kindly sang parts of it to me: old Balinese poetry is always sung. With a complete version in hand, I made whatever revisions to the structure seemed necessary and that suited what I had in mind.

For what I had in mind was to show the weird mix of the archaic and the modern that seemed to infuse Balinese reality at the time, and this was not part of the poem.

In the late 1980s, much of Bali was still largely an agrarian society and in many ways neolithic in its way of life: people still ploughed their rice fields with a cow, fetched water on their heads, cut whatever they needed from a nearby tree. The physical world was still scintillating with an invisible universe of spirits. Yet tourism and modern technology were introducing discordant notes. That didn't seem to faze the Balinese at all: they transported holy water in Coke bottles; they gave offerings to motorcycles and word processors; they joyfully electrified their magical rites with neon lights and loudspeakers — all with no thought of projecting the image of a spiritual society. They were innocent of a concern for appearances, which added greatly to their charisma.

It's an innocence that is beginning to fray.

When *The Painted Alphabet* was first published 1992, Bali's landscape was not as blotted out by chaotic building as it is today. But in fact the decay of the world is a concern of the Dukuh Siladri poem itself, which dates from at least as far back as the early twentieth century. Siladri is an ordinary villager who despairs at the evil abroad in the world and leaves home to live in a hermitage in the mountains. Asceticism is not the poem's message, however: evil pursues him there, too, and requires a response that is costly to his soul.

The structure of the story is generally true to the original poem; but to make space to weave in the dissonant elements and to build the story into a novel, I created back stories to fill out the characters, especially the villains, and created a few secondary characters as well. Thus, in the novel, the story of the junior witch Ni Klinyar begins before her reincarnation and tells of her (invented) overheated teenage parents. The back story of Klinyar's teacher and mentor, the arch-witch Dayu Datu, draws rather blithely on other Balinese myths, and her magical arts are full of deliberate anachronisms such as a Soviet airport lounge and a pony drowning in a swimming pool. And the temptation to deal with tourism was irresistible.

The contest of good and evil — or perhaps "order and chaos" is closer to the Balinese experience of these forces — is the issue at the heart of the Dukuh Siladri poem. But like its theatrical depiction, the discourse is not pious but full of joyful impudence. This is what I have tried to re-create in the novel.

ONCE UPON A TIME, deep in the heart of Bali in the village of Mameling, when life was still quiet and all things were in some way holy, each in its particular way, and the knowledge of the holiness of things was common knowledge, there were two brothers — the elder was called Siladri, and the other, Madé Kerti.

Bali then was a richly growing swarm in the world, humming with the afterclash of cymbals and gongs and slow soprano hand bells. It was a scented place. There was the perfume of mangoes and dung and frangipani, and the subtler scents of molds, hot wax on cloth, and woodsmoke on the skin of lovers. Bali was a shimmering world suspended between heaven and hell, and its people were operatic in their art, ferocious in war, and tender to their superiors, among whom were included not only princes and the humble, temple-sweeping priests, but also small children and the dead.

Ni Sabuk, the mother of Siladri and Madé Kerti, had no time for nonsense. She thought it nonsense to make pets of animals, for instance, or to dye one's hair, or to get in out of the rain. She disliked frenzy. If the ritual trance became too violent during mystery plays — with half-naked men sobbing and bending knives against their bellies — Ni Sabuk was unimpressed.

"Show-offs," she'd say, getting up in the middle of it all to go home.

"Where are my sandals?"

Ni Sabuk had been a widow as long as her sons could remember. Her husband fell dead of a stroke while helping her give birth to Madé Kerti. If anyone politely inquired how she'd lost her husband, she'd say, "He died in childbirth." As her sons grew, she provided for them by the careful management of their small rice fields and the weaving of fine cloth, which was highly prized by the local palace.

When Siladri presented Kadek to his mother as his bride-to-be, the girl was so frightened she could hardly speak.

Ni Sabuk sat cross-legged and bare-breasted at her loom in the shade of her high porch. Kadek stood next to Siladri and cringed in the sun. In a gesture of respect she pressed her hands together and raised them before her face. Ni Sabuk called for betelnut and scrutinized the girl over her spectacles.

"Who's your father, little one?"

Kadek told her his name (he was a modest farmer from a nearby village), then lifted her face toward the old lady and smiled.

Kadek did not know this, but her smile was like the sun breaking through clouds or the ringing of wonderful music — it was a falling in love. Ni Sabuk smiled back.

The three of them now sat together high in the shade of the porch. Trays of refreshments and betelnut were brought for them, and Kadek began to make a betel quid for the old lady. Siladri looked on, exultant. Kadek was still too heated with fear and happiness to speak; she just continued smiling as she wrapped the quid, enjoying the peppery scent of the leaf and the sensation of being so close to the origin of her lover. Her oval cheeks were flushed. Her teeth were big and even, like pale ivory game pieces. Ni Sabuk studied the girl. She looked at her big, soft lips, still lifted in that pretty smile, and guessed that the girl's vagina would also be voluptuous and articulate. On the other hand, her bones were too delicate.

"Can you weave?" said Ni Sabuk.

Kadek laughed. "Oh, no. I don't know how."

"Well, I'll teach you. Here, have some coffee. Siladri, give her some fruit, and some cakes — she's like a mosquito."

Ni Sabuk was pleased when Madé Kerti announced that he, too, would marry, having chosen Kadek's elder sister Rajin. Rajin was a lean, tough-minded, and competent girl who, unlike her sister, rarely smiled. The girls had lost their mother when Kadek was still a baby, and Rajin, at the age of nine, took on the woman's duties of the house. Life had made her handsome and austere.

Madé Kerti found her ravishing. The first time he went with Siladri to call on Kadek's father, Madé Kerti saw Rajin winnowing rice by the kitchen door, her headcloth wrapped loosely through her hair, shading her eyes. He could see only her fine nose and resolute mouth. Before Rajin noticed the guests, Madé Kerti admired her sinewy arms swirling rice in the circular tray, and instantly he fell in love.

Ni Sabuk was amused by the couple: Madé Kerti was as soft and jolly as Rajin was grave and spare. He worshipped his wife and always found an excuse to help her carry water, tend the animals, or sit with her as she made offerings. As for Rajin, she was comforted by the almost female quality of his company. It seemed to Ni Sabuk that the sharp edges of Rajin's nature were cushioned in the cocoon of Madé Kerti's love.

The household grew lively with two young wives now brightening the courtyard. They raised piglets and hens, and made rice cakes to sell at the market. Madé Kerti dug a garden bed for vegetables, where they grew chillies, spinach, and long climbing beans. By the wall of the house temple, Siladri planted a *cempaka* tree, whose waxy white flowers were precious for their scent, and the women tied these in their hair for their prayers.

Kadek blossomed in marriage; everyone could see it. As she went about her daily chores, she filled the courtyard with jokes and bits of song. She doted on her mother-in-law and enveloped her husband with the dizziness of love. She remained a respectful junior to her sister and grew to adore her brother-in-law.

All new love is esoteric. Siladri and Kadek lived for the privacy of night. One evening, as he was combing her hair in their room, Siladri said, "How is it that one God has so many names, my love?"

"How, b'li?" (*B'li* means older brother.)

"God has so many names that we can't possibly know them all. Every hair on your head has a different name of God, and every hair on Kerti's head has still a different name."

"And every hair on your head has yet a different name, but I think longer and grander," she whispered, smiling, and daring to touch the ends of his hair that fell just past his shoulders.

"And this has a name of God, too," he said, sliding his fingers over her lap, "but I can't pronounce it."

"Why not?" Bright-eyed, she held his hand to her lap.

"Because it's all vowels."

Kadek fell over, giggling. "And what about this?" She held up her hand like a bird-of-paradise flower, pointing to his genitals.

"Oh, that has a short, nasty name," Siladri flirted.

"I think it can have a long, heavy name," said Kadek. She giggled with her eyes.

"A long, liturgical name," murmured Siladri, growing heavy. Kadek, half laughing, half singing, began to chant a parody of an important hymn. Siladri grabbed her softly by the nape. "Naughty girl, you can't use that. You have to make up something new. Come on … right now …"

"I can't!" More laughter.

"Come on. Something processional. All right, never mind. Come here, and afterward I'll tell you why all the names of God add up to one. Really. Why are you laughing? *Naughty* girl …"

And so on.

But afterward Kadek was spread out in a deep, child-like sleep and could not see Siladri lying in the dark, staring upward, groping for the single name of God.

Ni Sabuk taught Kadek the *rejang* dance, the stately and repetitious temple dance performed by young girls and old women. She often commanded Kadek to dance for her, especially when Kadek had become too heavily pregnant to sit for long at the loom. "It's good for you," the old lady would say, knowing such things. "Just don't tell anyone." Ni Sabuk loved to watch her dance. She savored the girl's angular grace and loved to see Kadek's skinny arm stretching in a wide arc to the ground, her hands and feet like slim flags and her face raised in a radiant grin.

Kadek fitted Siladri like gold leaf to a royal statue. Although Ni Sabuk knew it, Kadek did not realize at first that he was a difficult, anxious man. Her eyes were full of lifelong promises every time she cooked or lifted a water jug to her head. Pregnant, she was like a little sail boat running before the wind. That Siladri was sensitive and restless she understood to be associated with the books.

Siladri had inherited from his father a large collection of palm-leaf books, which were stored in a cabinet in the house temple. The pages were fragile and required regular transcribing. During Kadek's pregnancy, Siladri spent much of his time at this, cutting the curly Balinese script into the palm strips with a tiny knife, then caressing ink into the incisions. Soon he found that he needed eyeglasses.

The books attracted a number of elderly literati, and Siladri began to stay up late into the night with them, smoking and taking turns reading aloud.

The texts were sacred poems written in Kawi, the old classical language that had come from the courts of central Java centuries before, and they exacted a certain formality: the reader would chant these verses in a large voice and specified meter, pausing every few lines; his "second" would then intone an improvised and equally mannered translation in Balinese. This rather stiff procedure was often interrupted while the readers chuckled over the profundity of a point or someone else made a suggestion about the phrasing of a certain passage. Kadek served the men coffee and betelnut, and sat dozing at a respectful distance. Sometimes Ni Sabuk sat at the edge of the circle, cutting and assembling coconut leaves for offerings

— the eternal and unhurried work of Balinese women — her hands moving automatically, her old face soft and distant as she followed the unwinding of the poetry.

It was through reading the holy books that Siladri found companionship in the feeling that something was very wrong with the world.

Siladri's elderly friends readily agreed, as older people always have, that the world was becoming an increasingly hellish place. They talked of the rise of insolence among young people, the growing carelessness about ritual protocol, the rumors of unsavory little wars.

They tried to explain things in terms of historical inevitability. They spoke of Kali Yuga, the dark phase in the turning agelessness of the world, the phase that always precedes the destruction of the world before fresh creation. They spoke mildly of the ills of the world from this vast perspective, but they illustrated their points with examples that caused twinges of alarm and disgust.

"My daughter-in-law," began one man in the flat tones of confession, "said something to me last week that makes me pray for a heart attack."

The others grew quiet, opening a clearing of attention. The man paused, feeling their permission to take time to choose his words. "She said to me, 'Father, you know, you could get a lot of money for those rice fields near the Ayung River.' I said to her, 'What would I do with a lot of money? And what would my grandchildren do without rice fields?' The silly woman said to me, 'Oh, but your grandson, if he had a minivan he could make so much money.' Always money. Can you understand this?" he said, opening his hands to show that there was no answer. "She speaks of rice fields and minivans in the same sentence."

There was a short silence, and then another man said simply, "My son has sold my kris."

A tug of shock passed through the company.

We must stop here for a minute to consider what a kris is, and why this news provoked a ripple of dread.

A kris is a long, snaky knife forged by priestly smiths according to formulas that remain to this day magical. As an instrument of murder and defense, it is marvelously tuned to its task. The wavy form of the blade cuts a broad swath of slaughter along its single vector. The metals comprising it are forged in a molecular weaving, alternating tissues of steel, bronze, silver, and gold, so that the surface is dappled: by polishing the blade, each of the ingredient metals are revealed in a controlled pattern. A cobra, by comparison, seems only a messy prototype of the kris — for there is also an incanted weapon sleeping invisibly within the kris, an unearthly force that is the spiritual signature of its owner. This signature, residing among the force fields of the enchanted metals, is so powerfully distilled that a man may send his kris to represent him as bridegroom in the ceremonies of marriage. A kris sometimes embodies the deified spirit of an ancestral king. Some say that to obtain possession of a man's kris, whether by theft or open victory, is not only to conquer the soul of that man but to monopolize an important spiritual resource of his entire family.

"My son has sold my kris," repeated the man, "to an art collector."

"A what?"

Siladri, who was younger than the rest, explained. "A foreigner. They'll buy anything — your front door, paintings, bits of walls —"

"My brother sold a painting the other day for the price of a male calf," another man said.

They all marveled at this, and agreed that the world was flying to pieces. The older men felt relieved that they would not, as they'd come to realize, live forever after all. They turned again to the holy texts and the nearer realms of life-after-death.

Kadek gave birth to a beautiful boy. They called him Mudita.

Siladri's heart rose and sank by turns in wonder at the birth of his son. He stared and stared at Kadek: a week before, she had been a pretty, pregnant girl who adored him; now she was the mother of a stranger. The sight of them enclosed in their holy circle filled him with fear — that they would die or forget him. He was afraid that love would drive him mad.

To distract himself, Siladri began to work on the design of a ring. He modeled beeswax around his finger and then spent days shaping and refining the wax with his writing knife until it seemed to him that the form was as perfect as he could make it. The design was fanciful: a tiger and a monkey circled the finger and met at the crown in a tangle of lines that formed the holy letter *ongkara*. Before taking the wax to be cast in gold, Siladri showed it to his family — first to Madé Kerti, who thought it a brilliant design and wonderfully executed, and then to his wife, who thought the same thing.

"This is for Mudita when he's grown," said Siladri. "It will fit him perfectly, since I have made it for my own finger."

One day soon after this, Rajin went into labor. Siladri himself went to the fields to call Madé Kerti home.

The sky was big over the rice fields, and all the sounds were muffled and distant: the clacketing of a bamboo rattle to scare away the birds; the stereo shriek of a kingfisher going by; the sound of children playing far below in the river ravine. The landscape was wide and calm, and Siladri soon spotted Madé Kerti grazing his ducks in the newly flooded fields. He was chasing a pair of stray ducklings, calling and splashing about in the water, so he did not hear Siladri at first. It was only when he finally straightened up, a baby duck in each hand, that he saw Siladri in front of him — an appearance that meant news.

"Oh!" said Madé Kerti, not knowing what to expect.

"Your baby is coming," said Siladri. "Let me help you with these other babies. You go ahead."

Madé Kerti hurried off, his soft flesh bouncing as he half ran. When he got home he found Rajin on a mat in their little room, drenched and gasping. Ni Sabuk sat behind her with the girl's head in her lap.

"Come here, Kerti, it won't be long now," said Ni Sabuk.

Madé Kerti crouched behind Rajin, supporting her back with his legs throughout her quick labor. As he held and pushed and wept with his wife, Ni Sabuk remembered Madé Kerti's birth, and she watched his face for telltale signs of exhaustion.

When the moon rose they were all murmuring over the perfect baby girl who would become the remarkable Kusuma Sari.

During the long, cool months of summer the two brothers drained their fields and let them grow over with soybeans. They watched their children grow more and more human and less like slumbering deities in transit from another world. The household was kept busy with the rites of passage that ease Balinese babies into life-on-earth.

"Have you ever noticed, Kerti," said Siladri, "that our children are like the rice cycle?"

"How's that?" said Madé Kerti. They were preparing for the ceremony to be conducted 210 days after Mudita's birth. "What do you mean, b'li?" he prompted Siladri, knowing how much his brother enjoyed a discourse.

"Well," said Siladri, "it's the same natural mathematics. Look at the intervals. We give our babies ceremonies at three days after birth, then twelve days, forty-two, one hundred and five, and then every two hundred and ten."

"Right!" said Madé Kerti. He was like a man moonstruck with love for his baby daughter.

"Right," said Siladri. "Now look at the rice cycle —"

Ni Sabuk laughed. "Siladri, the mathematical farmer," she said to herself.

Siladri laughed with her, but Madé Kerti grew impatient waiting to hear how Kusuma Sari was like the rice goddess.

"Go on, b'li. What about the rice cycle?"

"Same thing. We give ceremonies to the rice when we plant, and again when the rice comes into grain, and again when she's mature."

"And then the harvest," said Ni Sabuk.

Siladri's face was grave. He was thinking: Seed. Grain. Child. Harvest. God.

He was also thinking: Earth. Number. God.

The rain that year was late in coming, and as the earth grew dry and hot, people became knotted in themselves, and snappish. Village gossip took a mean turn, and there were whispers of weird tragedies.

"Kerti, I heard an awful story from the widow egg-seller today," said Siladri.

"Oh, the widow egg-seller is a witch," said Madé Kerti. "Don't listen to her."

"Well, perhaps she is. She certainly smells like one." Such was the pervasiveness of ill temper that even these two good men were affected. "Anyway, I hope she was lying. She said that Merta's daughter — you know, she married that blacksmith from Buleleng — gave birth to twins. Dead. They were strangling each other. I can't get it out of my mind."

"So why do you tell me?" said Madé Kerti, annoyed. "Now it's on my mind."

Siladri stopped as if struck. "Oh." Then, "Oh, Kerti, forgive me, that was selfish."

"Never mind, it's the season." Madé Kerti stared into the middle distance.

"The old people say it's Kali Yuga," said Siladri.

"The beginning of the end of the world?"

"Yes." Siladri was tired with the heat.

Madé Kerti sighed and turned to face his brother. "Well, they're probably right. This morning there was a mess in front of the palace. A serving girl got thrown out for hitting a princess in the face."

Siladri was shocked. He thought of Kadek's face, upturned and open and dazzled.

Madé Kerti lowered his eyes. "This serving girl, they threw her out stark naked. Her brother was there — he went crazy. Attacked the gate with his bicycle."

"His bicycle?"

"Well, you know, he just went wild, screamed the most incredible things." Madé Kerti paused, graying a bit. "They got him, of course."

The two brothers sat there in the heat for a few minutes, very still.

"What do you mean 'got him'?" said Siladri. "Killed him?"

There was a sharp clack from Ni Sabuk's loom.

Madé Kerti said, "No, no. Arrested him."

"And the girl?" said Siladri.

"Rode off on the bicycle," said Ni Sabuk.

A short, gingerly laugh passed around them.

This song was heard floating from the room of Siladri and Kadek one night:

"And my love," sang Siladri.

"And my love," sang Kadek.

"Is so great."

"Is so great," she sang.

"It can never end."

"It can never end, never end, it can never end."

SILADRI COULD NOT shake off his dis-ease with the world. As the rainy season finally broke, there were epidemics of insanity and rashes and scandal; rumors of witchcraft swarmed, and the village became a bog of slander. Siladri's nostrils were constantly pinched in disgust. His distress persisted after the spring equinox when the weather cleared, and found no relief in the balmy days of summer. He spoke to his mother about it.

"Mémé, it's like watching leprosy eat my hands and feet," he complained.

Ni Sabuk lifted her brows, considering her son over the edge of her spectacles. She gave him a small smile. "You're too sensitive. You feel everyone else's pain more than they do, just like your father. And where's he now," she said, not asking. "You should learn to meditate," she continued, in that tone of voice people now use to say, you should take vitamins. "And go to the fields with Kerti sometimes. Not all the world is so ugly." She smiled at him again, this time slowly, filling her eyes with him.

The next morning before dawn, Siladri went to the fields with his brother. The big waning moon still hung in the west and the air was pink; the vegetation was drenched in lavender light. Siladri felt the clean air chilling his nostrils, and he thought: This is the holiest of hours. To think that this happens every day! — and other such thoughts of the tourist of the dawn.

Siladri followed Kerti through the back lanes of the village. Here and there a kitchen fire glowed through the slats of woven bamboo walls; the roosters were already networking. The men crossed through mixed groves of banana, papaya, and yam, and skirted stands of bamboo with their likelihood of snakes. As they walked along, Siladri watched the easy and ordinary way of his brother's walking. Such a farmer — a hoe balanced on his shoulder and a scythe tucked into the back of his sarong. Madé Kerti's plump hips looked strong and graceful as he walked, and his fat feet trod surely over the ground. Siladri felt squeezed with love, and not knowing what to say, sang out: "Madé Kerti, king of the morning mists!"

Kerti gave a jiggly chuckle and turned to smile at Siladri, syncopating his stride to duck a branch of green tangerines.

They clambered down a steep ravine to the river and crouched in the cold stream, releasing the poisons of the night. They gasped as they sloshed water over their faces, necks, and armpits. In voices loud with cold, they shouted made-up mantras that echoed upward from the deep ravine. Madé Kerti began:

> Holy guardian of the spring,
> I offer you my nose and toes
> And everything.

Siladri picked up the warble:

> Take my brother's nose, that's fine.
> And please take his clothes,
> But leave me mine.
> Amen, amen, amen.

For a while they sang luxurious mischief together. They improvised — the chilly electricity of the river filling their heads with song — and they grinned at each other as the echoes enriched their harmony. Then they strode out of the water and stood naked and shivering on the bank. They dried themselves with their sarongs and glanced at each other's penises, recoiled from the cold into shy little knobs. Damp and exhilarated by their bath, they climbed back up the ravine to find daylight breaking over the world.

All the world was lifting, in mist and shapes of trees and the carved geography of the rice fields. A migration of herons cut an immense V slowly across the sky. Siladri and Kerti paused to send silent greetings to them and then continued walking until they came to their own fields, un-demarcated from their neighbors'.

The fields had recently been planted again, and for five silent hours they pulled weeds and wildflowers from between the rows of young rice.

When the sun was high and the air crashing with bouncing white light, they rested in the shade of a hut at the edge of their fields. They could smell the damp grasses of the roof drying in the sun. Siladri watched a stream of black ants staking out a visionary city around the contours of the hut, and his distress began to tick.

That evening, Siladri came home with the smell of meadows in his hair and a decision in his heart.

As soon as they finished eating, he asked Kadek to retire early with him. He had rehearsed the conversation all the way home, and for a while it went as he'd imagined it.

"Little sister, we are going to go live in the mountains," said Siladri as they sat up on their bed.

"The mountains? Why?"

"I think it's safer for you. There are terrible things going on these days — don't ask me to tell you about them, because I won't — but I'm convinced that we will have a better life away from all this — oh, a much, much better life!" Siladri paused; he knew that he wasn't being entirely candid. Kadek was sitting very straight, blinking at him, her mouth closed in a heap at the bottom of her face. Mudita was asleep in a warm bundle between them.

Siladri began again. "I have made a decision that I hope you will understand." He sounded like a stranger to himself and tried once more. "Kadek, I have decided to go to Gunung Kawi and ask the holy man Mpu Dibiaja to accept me as his pupil. I mean to stay. Please come with me. It will be a very simple life, but a worthy one."

"The *mountains*?" said Kadek again. "But where will we live?"

She was trying to form a picture of a kitchen in the mountains: the walls were only big branches and there was no roof — she'd look up and see only a towering malevolent tree that hid gloating giants and pestilential birds and tigers that could read her thoughts.

Siladri took her hand. "We'll ask Mpu Dibiaja to let us live in his household. Kadek, please trust me. My dear little kitten, my little hen, I wouldn't let anything happen to you. We'll be taking a path of holiness. We'll be protected. As long as we're together we have everything we need."

Kadek would not look at him.

"The true world," he continued rather pedantically, "isn't things or places, it's love."

"Then why are we going?"

"It's like this: I must do this. If you come with me, that would make me very happy. I love you more than anyone on earth. But if it would make you unhappy to leave our village, then you may stay."

Kadek took down her hair and put it up again. Her heart was kicking.

Then Siladri added, "But Mudita must stay behind. He must grow up here with Kerti."

Kadek got up abruptly and left their room. She walked out into the night toward the pigpen, intending to throw herself down in the mud and cry until her soul fled her body; but the sight of the black mud only made her feel more lost. She went instead into the kitchen, her own cocoon and realm. She let herself fall onto the kitchen platform, among sacks of rice and baskets of roots and half-finished offerings. Dry sobs pinched her chest, but the tears wouldn't come. She got up and washed her face from the spring jar in the corner, hoping the water would coax along her tears, but it only made her more starkly awake. Reality was never so sharp: Siladri was leaving to become an ascetic in the wilds of the mountains. Mudita, their baby, was to be left behind. What would she do?

Kadek took some ears of corn that were drying on a beam and began to pop the kernels into a basket. She needed to be busy to think. The kernels clicked into the basket, and soon they made an agreeable heap of orange beads. She worked quickly and rhythmically, humming flatly and swinging her legs a bit, her mind stilled to a wordless thread. She pulled down more corn from the rafters and clicked on.

And then she began to think about the mountains. She had been to the mountains once, on a long pilgrimage with her village. She was still a little girl then, and Rajin had told her that they were securing the soul of their mother. The band of villagers had walked for days, sleeping in temples and villages along the way.

For the first day they had walked north, and uphill. As the land grew higher and more wild, they left behind the soothing vistas of rice fields and the free-form plantings of familiar crops like coconut, banana and papaya. They passed inky clumps of sago palms and spiky salak trees. Sometimes their path took them through stretches of wild forest where the only sound was the wind. The procession's drum-and-cymbal orchestra would start up then, conjuring a shield of noise. Strange fowl scuttled in front of them. The smells were clear and savory and lonely.

On the second day they began walking northeast, descending and ascending river gorges that fell away into the bright green air. Kadek's legs quivered with fatigue, but she dared not say anything unless someone else complained first; but no one did, not about being tired. The villagers worried about slim green snakes and the possibility of meeting a tiger, although tigers had become rare by then; but they were more frightened of running into a monkey or a piglet, for these could be the guise of a sorcerer abroad on an assignment; or of meeting a wandering corpse who had been improperly buried and was hungry, or the guardian demon of some grove or spring whom they'd startled, or a cloud of illness gathering force at a crossroads.

For the rest of her life Kadek bore at the nape of her neck a fear of the mountains.

But could she let Siladri go alone? It would be like allowing him to disappear into living death. And where would that leave her?

If she stayed behind, she would be living in a state of ambiguous widowhood, a long life of loss and uncertainty, always wondering if her husband was alive, if he was well or ill, wondering if he remembered her. Should she not follow him? He had said that she might; even a holy man needed a wife to comb the twigs from his hair, to fetch water and gather flowers for his prayers. Who else was she but his wife?

And as for Mudita, he was Siladri's son and must take Siladri's place; she knew that to be the true order of the world. The thought of being separated from her baby crushed her ribs together and at last she began to cry, because she had already come to realize that she would leave Mudita behind. At least he would be safe and well protected with Madé Kerti and her sister. He would become a fine young man, with a fine gold ring and, one day, his father's land. And perhaps — although she wasn't sure how it was with holy men — perhaps they would have another son, a mountain son who would be at home in that world and teach her to be unafraid.

By the time she finished with all the corn, the night had grown cold and everything was still. Dawn was several hours away. Kadek's teeth chattered, but she was calm. She knew now what she would do, and she went back to join her husband.

The next night, Siladri called Madé Kerti to join him for a quid of betelnut.

It was already late, and the old waning moon was just beginning to rise. They settled on the veranda of the western pavilion to watch its progress through the trees.

Siladri didn't know how to begin, so he said nothing. Madé Kerti settled into the peacefulness of the night, and after a while he began to chuckle to himself. He said, "You know, my Kusuma Sari — where does she come from, I wonder. You know what she did today? She was playing in the middle of the courtyard — the middle, you see, no trees around — and she put her little hands up in the air and, do you know, a six-petaled frangipani just dropped into her hands. Not five but six petals! She has genius, Siladri, like her mother." Madé

Kerti laughed happily at his great good luck.

Siladri smiled and then, sinking under what he was about to say, spoke abruptly: "Kerti, I'm leaving."

Madé Kerti's laughter evaporated and he turned his head toward Siladri, his mouth slowly dropping to a judicial frown. "What do you mean, you're leaving? Leaving what?"

"All of it. This world. You." Siladri's eyes grew hot. "I'm going to the mountains to meditate and I won't be coming back."

Siladri paused to light a fat clove cigarette, and Madé Kerti waited.

"The world is old and dirty," Siladri said, "and I cannot bear to be in it any longer. Look at what's going on around us: virtuous old men being robbed by their children; ordinary people trying to be aristocrats, and aristocrats behaving like thugs. And the most unspeakable sorts of other things — you know what I mean. It's a perfect world for criminals and the rich, and God is practically invisible. I want to live differently. That is, I want to learn to live differently. Can you understand this, Kerti? I hope very much that you will understand."

Madé Kerti reached for a betel quid. His fingers were quivering with alarm, and suddenly he didn't know any words. He stared at the horizon, backlit by the aging moon. He searched the shapes of the trees for prompting.

"B'li," said Madé Kerti. "This world, you say, is filling up with evil. Maybe you're right. But where, except in this world, do we belong?"

"Do you feel as if you belong in this world?" asked Siladri, deadly curious. He peered hard at Kerti.

"I do," said Madé Kerti. He stared at his brother, trying to imagine how it must feel not to belong to life.

"And what is this world, then, that you belong to?"

"Well," said Madé Kerti, "you know." He cast around. "Taking care of things. Taking care. You know — Mémé, the children, the land. The village. Our ancestors. Come on, you know perfectly well."

"The Dharma," Siladri summarized.

"That's right, the Dharma … isn't it? Anyway, it's all we've got, this world. Until we die. I think …" He faded off, genuinely unsure. Siladri wanted to pick up his brother in his arms like some big soft puppy.

"Good men like you, Kerti, do belong in the world."

"And so do you," said Madé Kerti, becoming angry. "You have responsibilities here. You have a family, there's the village, the temples." He wiped his hand over his face. "I don't understand, I'm sorry. Really. I don't know. Maybe I just don't want you to leave."

"I wouldn't leave for anything but heaven," said Siladri, "but I must. I'm absolutely decided. I will go to Gunung Kawi to study with Mpu Dibiaja, the hermit saint. I mean to learn to live in the mind of God."

Madé Kerti twitched. "I'm frightened for you. I think this is … I'm sorry, I think this is dangerous. That is, I think you're inviting some kind of danger. I feel it."

"Danger?" said Siladri. "You don't mean lions and tigers?"

"No, of course not," said Madé Kerti, privately adding lions and tigers to his growing anxiety. Indeed, he did not know what he meant, or what the danger was that he felt.

"Now listen, Kerti. I'm making you head of the household. Everything I have is yours. I know that you will take care of everything and everyone very well."

"You've already talked to Kadek about this?"

"Yes, she's coming with me."

"But what does she think, our Kadek? She agrees with this?"

Siladri picked his words carefully. "She won't let me go alone."

"And you'll take Mudita, of course — to the mountains." Madé Kerti was seized by the strangeness of it all.

Siladri busied himself with crushing his cigarette. "I want you to raise my son."

And now Madé Kerti felt that all logic and sense were whipped from under his feet, and he burst out sobbing, rocked by the upset in the order of his world. He raised his face and wept aloud in a deep, honking baritone. Siladri, shattered, wiped his brother's cheeks and couldn't think of anything to say. Was holy life to be like this?

Madé Kerti's wife, Rajin, appeared in a doorway behind them, a sarong wrapped around her shoulders. She sat down a short distance from her husband. Siladri continued, including Rajin without looking at her.

"In eleven days' time I will leave with Kadek. Kerti, you will take my place here. I'm leaving Mudita with you so that he can help you when he's grown. You will be a good father to him, I know, and I hope he will be a good son to you in return. He seems to have his mother's sweetness." Siladri reached for another cigarette. "Please let's not discuss this again after tonight. My decision is fixed." And then he added, with a gasp, "But I will miss you very much."

Rajin, leaning against a post in the shadows, was quiet and her face was stern, but she wiped tears from her face with her wrist. She had experienced so many different kinds of pain that it didn't occur to her to intervene.

Siladri continued. "Explain to Mudita, when he's old enough to understand, that his father went to the mountains to live in the nature of God. Give him this ring and tell him that I made it for him. If ever he wants to find me, he can find me with this."

That made perfect sense to Madé Kerti and his wife.

"So then," said Siladri, "so that's it." They all sat for a while, no one speaking, each letting the others be alone with their thoughts. The moon now was high overhead and so bright in the courtyard that they could make out the pink of the hibiscus, and the frangipanis glowed frozen white. They saw Ni Sabuk make her way carefully across the yard to the kitchen, ignoring them.

"Am I head of the household now?" said Madé Kerti.

"Yes, if you like."

"Then you will take Kusuma Sari with you." Rajin started, but Madé Kerti held up his hand. "To remind you of us, and of my love for you. She won't be any trouble. Kadek can nurse her. When you are old, Kusuma Sari will take care of you."

And in that way, the two brothers exchanged children. Then slowly, they all retired for the night.

As Rajin walked back to the room where she slept with her baby and her husband, she felt her world convulsing. Madé Kerti came in shortly and found her sitting in the farthest corner of their cot. She whirled on him when he touched her arm, and her fine teeth gleamed in the moonlight, but when she saw his face awash with tears, her anger crumbled and she took his big head in her arms. For a long time they rocked and wept and clung to each other, their hot faces buried in each other's neck, too wretched to speak. Eventually, exhausted by their weeping, they began to tidy their thoughts and faces with words.

Rajin took Madé Kerti's hair in her fingers and held his swollen face away from her own. "I know you adore your brother," she began. Fresh big tears slid down his cheeks. This made her furious all over again: "But why must you give away our baby? Is this how you're going to run our house? Maybe tomorrow you'll give Mudita to the widow egg-seller!"

Madé Kerti straightened, and there was a glint about him as he looked at his wife. "Rajin, this is a catastrophe. You know there's only one way to behave."

"What's that?" she said, challenging him.

" 'Good thoughts, good words, good actions.' At least, well, maybe that way we won't make stupid mistakes. Let Kusuma Sari go with Siladri. This is a loving thing to do. It will remind him that there is also goodness in our ordinary world."

Rajin was quieted by this. Madé Kerti caressed her neck.

"You're very sad," he said, "and so am I — so what? Of course we are, it can't be helped. What else? Siladri wants to become a holy man. He can't help that either."

Rajin began to reel under all that couldn't be helped. "But our baby girl living in the forest with that madman —"

Madé Kerti put his arms around her, pulled her onto his lap, and said, "Now, now. He's right, in a way. The world is changing, and who knows what things will be like by the time she's a young woman? In the mountains she'll become strong and healthy with pink cheeks. And she'll be well brought up in the house of Mpu Dibiaja. I've heard a little about him. They say the place is comfortable and kind, with big gardens and lots of animals. I feel that she'll be happy there. And anyway, just look at our Kusuma Sari — does she look worried?"

Indeed, Kusuma Sari lay fast asleep with a smile parting her lips, as if she were listening to some inner music. Both her parents saw a delicious white light around her. Perhaps it was only the moonlight, but perhaps not: it seemed to rise in a hum and wrap around her. In any case, both her parents were, from that moment on, confident of the safety of Siladri and Kadek, as long as Kusuma Sari was with them. From that moment, too, all their love was freed to lavish on Mudita.

Ni Sabuk accepted Siladri's plan with no argument and almost no comment. She simply listened to her sons and daughters-in-law with a nod and a smile as they each privately tried to gain her sympathy. She knew it would be divisive to respond singly to any one of them, and as to her private feelings, she had long ago discarded them as irrelevant.

All she ever said (and this to Siladri) was, "Mpu Dibiaja is a good man. I knew him years ago. He was a friend of your father's. If anyone can teach you anything, he can. Listen to him. Let me give you a piece of cloth for him, to take as a gift. And you'll need something warm for Kadek. Kusuma Sari will be fine."

On the morning of their departure, the family sat together for the last time for formal prayers in the house temple. These were conducted by a local priest, a very old and tiny man dressed all in white. Ni Sabuk attended to him with a large white cloth wrapped around her middle. The priest pronounced long mantras and steadied their prayers with the single silvery ringing of his hand bell. The family sat with trays of flowers and incense sticks jabbed in the ground before them. One by one they picked up a blossom and, passing it through a waft of incense, raised it to their foreheads, holding it in their fingertips and sending their prayers on the carriage of flowers and mantra and scented smoke — for that is how the gods of Bali are addressed. First a red blossom to Bhatara Guru; then a white one to Bhatara Iswara; then a yellow one to the gods of Gunung Agung; then the complex and lovely little *kwangen* — a neat conical packet containing flowers, coins, and traces of betelnut and ornamented with the complicated shapes of long-forgotten syllables cut into young coconut leaves — this raised with a stick of incense and addressed to the gods of their house temple, the ancestral guardians of the family. The ringing of the hand bell widened over their house.

As they roused from their prayers, the priest turned and sprinkled them with holy water. He picked a blossom from the beaker of water for each of them to tuck behind an ear or tie into their hair. Kadek, with Kusuma Sari in her lap, placed a rose petal behind both the baby's ears and returned Rajin's smile with a big grin.

At the gate there was boisterous well-wishing and a loose swarm of friends, neighbors, and onlookers as Siladri and Kadek, carrying the baby Kusuma Sari, set out through the village and onto the open road. The crowd was dense with opinion, some of it unfriendly.

"I don't know what they're running away from."

"Bought by witches, I heard."

"People shouldn't talk about what they don't know," said someone to the air in front of his face. "He's following his heart to God. What's wrong with that?"

"Well, God bless them — who knows?"

At the back of the crowd a young couple slipped away into a nearby grove, leaving behind a faint smell of burning human hair.

WE SHALL SEE presently what becomes of the children of Siladri and Madé Kerti. In the meantime, there is another child who will figure in our story a bit later, a dangerous and weirdly gifted little girl, Ni Klinyar.

At the time when Siladri and Madé Kerti were marveling over the fingers of their babies, Klinyar was slumbering in the netherworld, as yet unborn, more subtle than a virus, not yet even virtual plasma, perhaps only the tropism of an idea beneath the sleep of the gods. While Siladri was fashioning his ring for Mudita, a strange constellation was forming in the realm of ancestral decisions. The soul of Klinyar was about to be sentenced to reincarnation.

The decadence of our times precludes our understanding matters of such a divine nature — unless, perhaps, we are armed with the chisels of mathematics. To report on the circumstances leading to the incarnation of Ni Klinyar, we must do as human children do and make dolls of our ideas — we must anthropomorphize. (But, because we are no longer innocent, we must remember to prayerfully apologize beforehand, invoking the saintly patronage of Sang Hyang Aji Saraswati to intercede in the shaping of our effigies.)

At this moment, the orbit of the soul of Klinyar gives off a searing whine, and the gods are keen to have her incarnate soon: in the netherworld as in life, she is disruptive. Her repeated delinquencies have brought her again and again to the judicial bench of Bhatara Yama, the Lord of Dharma, before whom she has appeared each time as unrepentant as a diamond. Each time, she was relegated to a darker dimension of hell, only to burn more viciously invulnerable to its punishment. When she joined in the torturing of the other souls of the damned, Bhatara Yama called on the Great God Shiva to intervene.

"Even among the damned, my Lord, she is corrosive," said the God Yama. "She regards suffering with sarcasm."

"Bring her to me, good Yama."

Then the God Shiva condensed himself into a steep violet vacuum, sonorous and vast. From the periphery of this heavenly field of force came a thin, screaming line, and the soul of Klinyar was hurtled into its midst.

Nothing in the midst of nothing.

For a long while there was only stasis as the soul of Klinyar lay inert in the heart of God. Eventually there arose a swelling tension, a deepening and drawing away, leaving the soul of Klinyar suspended — a single ingredient of glow bobbing uncertainly, without vector.

The God Shiva substantiated further, condensing around Klinyar until he became a swarming brightness, and his single sound shattered into a shimmering array of high, bell-like tones. The soul of Klinyar, too, swelled in rapid complication, until at last they rested face to face in a state of radiant plasma — Klinyar in the form of an embryonic curl, and the Lord God Shiva in the shape of a perfect rose. Tendrils of light connected them, and they began to converse.

"Now Klinyar, do you know that even hell is in the embrace of heaven?"

There was a silence, then a tiny buzz and the smell of sulfur.

"Klinyar, I have a plan for you. I want you to grow," said the God Shiva. Klinyar yanked against her tether of light until it became a thread, and then only a strand of photons. The petals of the rose lifted lightly, and the ray became a vine that gathered Klinyar curling back to a comfortable distance before the rose. The God's voice was like scent. "Hell is not challenging enough for you. You need refining. We're going to send you back to life-on-earth."

"No no no no no." Klinyar sobbed and gagged miserably.

"Are you afraid, my tiny ogre? Everybody's afraid going in and out. But you've done this before. You know you always arrive."

"Oh, my Lord, it's not just that. I'm not good at being there. It weighs too much. I'm wanting all the time. It hurts there. Everything I do, they stop me."

The God Shiva murmured to Klinyar. "I know, I know. That's exactly the way it is. This time it will be a little different for you. There's a special part for you, just as you are." The God did not add that it is always that way. "And this time, I will be close to you. Not with you, but close. You will be alone like everyone else, but if you need me and if you call upon me, I will come to you and help you."

"Ridiculous!"

"And I will show you how you can help us," continued the Lord God from deep inside the rose.

"Lies! Dead teeth! Stinking peony! Broken radio!" And so on.

At this, the Lord Shiva burst into long, happy peals of laughter, fluttering the petals of the rose. The laughter calmed, and the God said, "Oh, Klinyar," and then began laughing again, the rose rocking with hilarity. "This is going to be good," he said with a high-pitched sigh, and started laughing all over again.

"Whinnying idiot!" Klinyar's screeching blasphemy rolled on. The Lord God continued to chuckle for a moment.

"My little Klinyar. You still have all the world to understand. I am all the world. And so are you. Now back to school and work that out. I'm sending you to Bali. It's not quite so remote from us."

Then there was a marvelous explosion. The soul of Klinyar was hurtled deep into obscurity, where it lay mute, pushed helplessly down through the double-helix road on the peristaltic journey toward birth. Klinyar would not recall this private audience with the Lord of Lords until many years later, but it left an iridescence that Klinyar carried from birth, much to the consternation of her parents.

SILADRI AND KADEK took turns carrying Kusuma Sari, sharing the delight of the bright-eyed, warm-smelling child. They fell into nonsense songs as they held her, bumping and skipping to coax a bubbling of laughter from her. Kadek was still in full milk, and when they stopped near midday in the shade of a tree, she nursed her niece, her oval face warm with contentment. By sunset they'd come to a high plateau from which they gazed out over the hills and all the way to the sea. They ate some fruit from their basket and shared a cigarette. Soon they made for a nearby village to request shelter for the night.

The next day as they moved into higher country they pointed out to each other the wild-growing herbs that they knew only from the medicine sellers at the markets, the sudden clouds of butterflies, and the closeness of songbirds. The people they met were sturdier, and there seemed to be many children at work alongside their parents — little boys carrying big scythes and little girls carrying great bundles of firewood on their heads.

People stopped what they were doing to greet them and to inquire, with wide open faces and the most courteous language, where they were going, where they were from, and whatever else they could think of to engage the young couple in conversation. After they'd passed, the mountain people continued to discuss these things among themselves.

Kadek enjoyed these encounters and the pleasure of exchanging familiar greetings with anyone they met. She was full of all that surrounded her. The air up here was big and fresh, and the light seemed drenched with color. The water running through the ditches and streams they crossed was colder and clearer than anything she'd ever experienced. There was a smell of woodsmoke and bitter grass in the air. Kadek began to think that her fear of the mountains was perhaps a childish residue, that when she'd followed her sister's hips on that long pilgrimage as a child, she'd been too little and still too stupid to see what was actually around her. Now she took in the broad world with appetite. She chatted with the girls who followed them as they skirted villages.

"Is that your husband?"

"Yes, isn't he handsome?" (Lots of giggles.)

"Is that your baby?"

"Yes. This is Kusuma Sari."

"Is that real gold, your earrings?"

"No," she'd say, lying with aplomb like a lady, "just fake."

"Give them to me?"

"Do you live around here?" she'd ask, turning the conversation. "Your mothers must be very pretty, because you're the prettiest girls I've seen all day." (More giggles, shyer manners, urgent appeals to come visit their houses.)

Siladri inquired of the farmers he met the way to Gunung Kawi. Kadek watched him in these conversations, admiring his graciousness and proud of his discretion whenever he was asked, as he inevitably was, why the honorable stranger was going to Gunung Kawi.

"I want to pay my respects to a friend of my father." And inevitably this was met with a bow, and the farmer would accompany them for several hours through his land.

Sometimes in the evenings delicate fogs rose from the valleys, veiling the trees in a chill and fragile flatness so that they looked like queer characters on a screen of old silk.

Time became lost, and Kadek began to wonder if they weren't moving in a wide circle. She grew tired and absent-minded, and lost count of the days they'd been in the high, smoke-scented country.

One afternoon a breathlessness came over them, and they stopped in a high field and saw the western mountains spread flat across the distance like a violet cut-out. A storm stood over the plains to the southwest, and as they watched it flicker and climb, they noticed the cool shift in the composition of the air around them. All color drained away, and there was a feeling of the world closing down.

Siladri steered them to the lee of a courtyard at the far side of the field, and then, realizing that they would be directly in the path of the storm, he hurried them to a nearby banyan tree, the massive fig tree that looms like a building and is the roosting place of spirits. Kadek balked at the sight of the magical tree, but Siladri pushed her forward at the small of her back.

"It's all right, it's all right. We'll be much safer here, and we'll have a good view of the storm." And so they crouched between the knees of the huge old tree and peered through its long-haired curtain of aerial roots and branches into the steely air. Kadek tucked Kusuma Sari into her shirt and fished around in the betelnut purse for the makings of a small offering to protect the baby, just in case, sealing it with the tiny florets of some flowering grasses by her feet.

Suddenly the light tilted and there was a vacuum gasp in the middle sky. Siladri and Kadek cringed toward each other as the storm began to bear down, advancing on the high hills like a vertical wall of marching voices. Paralyzed, they waited.

A rainless galloping in the air swooped up over the hills, knocking tall trees together and setting the young trees into convulsions. A drop in the light announced the first fat drops of rain marking out the territory to be assaulted; and then the rush of the full furious body of the storm firing into the ground, the walls, the innocent air, the big tree above them getting all mixed up in itself; and then all was drenched with the beating of flying water.

For some time the rain whipped and danced on its hind legs, and Kadek saw the swirling of the God Indra's chariots and felt the sting of the wet manes of war horses. Siladri, nailed against the tree by the downpour, felt his skin become as streaked as the bark; the rain ran down his face, around his nose, into his slightly open mouth. He watched the big thick jackfruit trees curling themselves in the milk of the storm. The branches of banana trees beat gong-like on a vertical pivot, and the coconut palms swirled their arms of shimmering fingers. Below in the ravine, bamboos were rioting. The whole world was bucking with rain. Then slowly a pearly haze rose from the earth as the rain slowed to a useful drumming, and gradually moved on, pushing its dark future before it.

Siladri watched the fat broad yam leaves bobbing under big silver balls of water. In the shelter of the yams, fragile tendrils of weeds arched in a see-through green, as if writing questions; orchids poked up and yawned and blared astonishing purples. On the stone steps that now appeared in the courtyard wall, mosses seemed to ripple and cast off a quiet glow of contour. Siladri was agog. He let his legs slide forward and settle into the moving mud. Kadek, beside him, was emitting rapid little coughing sounds. Kusuma Sari was wide-eyed and solemn.

The afternoon light rose in an arabesque, and with a quick kick of western fire, faded into dusk. All was water-logged. Siladri began to stir his family. Kadek slumped in exhaustion and could not be roused. Siladri lifted the baby from her blouse and was surprised to find her still dry and clutching a betel quid. He plumped and poked Kusuma Sari and got her to play with his nose, but he was distressed to see Kadek sprawled against the tree, her clothes slippery with mud. Her pretty face was filthy and tucked into her neck, and she breathed with a tiny snore.

"'Dek 'Dek, let's go now. Come on, there's a big fine house nearby. Let's go, little pilgrim." But Kadek was icy and ill and would not move.

Siladri became very frightened. He dug out the cloth his mother had provided for Kadek and tucked it around her as well as he could. Kusuma Sari began to cry and squirm. Siladri clutched the baby and stared at the gate of the house, silently begging for help to appear.

The light leached away, and Siladri cowered amid the tree roots, weak with shame — cold, wet, and mud-smeared, with his brother's fretting baby in his arms and his brave young wife collapsed, perhaps dangerously ill. He would go up the gate and ask for help at the house.

He must go: it was almost night. He stirred and tried to stand up, but the sight of Kadek lying mud-splattered against the tree made him sink back to the ground as if tethered. He couldn't leave her alone like that.

Kusuma Sari began to cry in earnest now, the full-hearted abject crying of babies that wrings their whole bodies and makes their faces horrible with grief. Hot tears squeezed out from the corners of her eyes, and Siladri thought he had never heard such despair. It caught him in his chest and tugged at his face.

Just then a lamp, and then an old man, appeared at the gate in the stone wall, a small old man with large ears protruding from under his white headcloth and a merry, ironic face. The old man peered at Siladri and made his way over to the tree.

"Now, who's that sitting here, and how is it that his wife is dead?"

Siladri stared up into the face of Mpu Dibiaja.

— What dead?

Siladri turned to Kadek. She was absolutely still, her eyes not quite closed, a lock of hair pasted against the corner of her mouth. Siladri touched her dirty face. It was Kadek, but it was not. Siladri turned and looked up again at the old man. He was not Kadek. He looked back at the muddy dead girl. He thought: What has happened to my wife?

He turned to his mother — but it was Mpu Dibiaja. Siladri said, "I told her it would be all right. I told her I would take care of her," and then his face bolted out of control in a seizure of weeping. He crawled to Kadek, shaking his head and wailing, "Kadek, Kadek, my little flower face, oh my wife, how can you leave me like this?" Siladri took her in his arms and rubbed his face against hers and bit her lips and then shrank back as his teeth broke into her bloodless flesh. He called her in a high voice:

Where have you slipped away to?
Are you behind the tree?
Have you gone back to the village?

I know, you've gone back to the village!
You've gone back to get the baby,
It's because we forgot the baby,
Let's go back and get the baby,
And go to heaven all together,
Go to heaven all together,
You and the baby and me —

Mpu Dibiaja yanked Siladri up. "Siladri," he said, "get up before you eat that corpse away. Remember who you are." He took Siladri by the shoulders and shook him gently. "You have work to do. Your wife has died and your baby is crying. Now come here, child, and listen to me. Pick up the little one, that's right. She'll be fine. We have many friends here, wonderful friends, you will see. Oh, here they are already." Mpu Dibiaja smiled into the surrounding gloom.

Siladri saw nothing and could hear nothing but the beating of wings. Then a rustle, and the shocked face of a deer appeared. Siladri's skin jumped as he saw thudding up to the old man a full-grown tiger, one ear slightly cocked and grizzled with white hairs. Siladri, queer and icy with shock, thought: That must be an old service injury.

Very quickly they were surrounded by such a variety of animals that Siladri felt sure that he had already died. There was a fluttering of birds, a cool party of monkeys, a wild boar with huge improbable tusks and a very ugly wife, a family of deer. There was a lion — the dark-maned, racy type peculiar to Bali in those days — who kept his three females out of sight with a few lashes of his tail and then made way for the last arrival: a looming elephant who bore about his head an invisible jingling of bells.

Siladri, already reduced to a stupor, gaped unafraid. Mpu Dibiaja smiled again. Siladri looked at the old man and thought he had never seen such sweetness in a human face, not even in his own child. Mpu Dibiaja addressed the animals in the high language with which one addresses high priests, royalty, and newborn children: "My dear friends." And here his smile, his whole person, became so sweet, so deferential, that he seemed to give off a glow. "Thank you very much for coming. This is our friend Siladri, and right now he needs our help."

Siladri's head was ringing, but he noticed that Mpu Dibiaja was now seated on a large flat rock and that he himself was seated quite comfortably with him, slightly lower, to his right. It was all he could do to resist dropping his head on the old man's knee. Kusuma Sari, he noticed too, was asleep on his own lap, and Kadek lay peacefully under a bower of leaves. A warm light lifted outward and revealed the faces of the animals, guarded but attentive. What extraordinary charm this man has, Siladri thought stupidly. What an extraordinary day. Mpu Dibiaja looked at the animals assembled, as if silently tying a knot with each. The wild boar's sow flopped over on her side and began to snore. One of the younger male monkeys crossed his legs. The deer inched quietly forward, testing the air with their ears.

"This is my friend Siladri," Mpu Dibiaja said again. "Let's think of him from now on as my son." Siladri lowered his forehead to the old man's feet. Mpu Dibiaja rested his hand lightly on Siladri's head and continued confiding in the animals.

"My Siladri's young wife has died and wants to go home to the gods. And his little girl now needs a mother. Now, my friends, what can we do to help him?"

There was a slight shifting among the animals. A heavy female monkey elbowed her way to the front to get a better view of the disheveled Siladri. Mpu Dibiaja allowed the animals to settle down before continuing.

"First the dead, and first, too, the living." Then he murmured to Siladri, "What a thing it is to be a human being." He raised his voice and said to the animals, "My venerable friend Sang-Gadja-the-Elephant, it would honor us if you would lend your care to our travail, the cremation of my poor child's wife." He whispered to Siladri, "We have no *banjar* here, no village community to help in such times. Accept the labor of the beasts."

He turned again to the elephant, who was looking at Mpu Dibiaja with slow tenderness. "Sang Gadja, my good teacher, gather us firewood, I beg you, for a fast and hot fire to speed this lady to heaven. Marshal the birds to bring young coconut leaves and fresh flowers, and bid the cleverest mother monkeys to show us their skill in the making of offerings — we will remind them of what's required. My brother Sang-Singa-the-Lion will lead the way to the holy spring, where we will ask for clear water to carry our prayers. Sang Gadja, I beg you, when all is ready, to carry the young woman carefully to the cremation ground." He bent over to stroke Siladri's hair. "And also, Sang Gadja, throughout all the preparations, share with us your great heart, your exemplary concentration, and your ... your gift of grief."

Mpu Dibiaja then addressed the birds. "My exalted friends blessed with wings: please bring our deepest respects to the gods of Gunung Agung the Mountain-of-Our-Origins, and ask them to carry our prayers in vanguard on the journey of this good girl who was the wife of Siladri.

"Dear, good Sang-Cheleng-the-Wild-Boar, whose tusks never cease to frighten me: lend us your help as guardian of all these proceedings, and discourage what mischief may come from the ground to disrupt this holy work."

Mpu Dibiaja paused again and seemed to examine the rock on which he and Siladri were sitting as if he were considering buying it. Finally he said, "And let there be forthcoming one cub or chick or kid whose soul will fly cheek to cheek to heaven with this lady. You can work that out among yourselves, I think."

And then he tucked himself into himself and spoke as if to himself, softly and ever more softly, until at last all was quiet and dark around him.

Siladri began to feel the night mists heavy on his sleeves. He shifted his feet and felt the warm weight of Kusuma Sari in his arms. Mpu Dibiaja emerged from his communion and propped up an eyebrow.

"And now, the other first order of business," he said, "which is this baby. Her mother is dead. Let's try to help the little one live. Is there among us someone who would nurse this child?"

The animals stirred uncertainly, then deferentially. To Siladri's horror, there came forward a slinky young lioness. Mpu Dibiaja beamed, and gathered Kusuma Sari from Siladri's arms and offered her to the cocked jaws of the lion, who carried her a short distance and lay her on the ground. At the same time, there trotted forward a little doe who, with a quick curtsy to the lioness, bent her dainty attention to the bundled baby on the ground. Then together the lioness and the doe disappeared with the baby into the dark. Siladri stared and stroked his face. Mpu Dibiaja laid his hand on Siladri's knee and wrapped him in his smile.

"Bear with us. They're primitive, but good-hearted. All is well. And now you, my poor Siladri, won't you come into the house? We will prepare you a hot bath and something nice to eat, and tonight you will sleep in my house and be like a little baby yourself again."

With the animals guarding the corpse of Kadek and the two incongruous dams tending to Kusuma Sari, there seemed almost nothing left to do.

Almost. There was a tendril-like nagging in Siladri's heart, a sensation very low and faint, like the urge to urinate in sleep. Siladri looked at Mpu Dibiaja with open, empty eyes; he could find no words.

"Ah!" said Mpu Dibiaja and settled Siladri into the cross-legged prayer position. Mpu Dibiaja took Siladri's hands into his own and pressed them together above his forehead — just as Ni Sabuk had done when Siladri was cutting his first teeth, teaching him to pray — and he coached Siladri in this childhood prayer that knows no limits of time or space:

> *Father-Mother-God,*
> *Loving me,*
> *Guard me while I sleep,*
> *Guide my little feet up to Thee.*

IN THE VILLAGE OF MAMELING, where Mudita was learning to help Madé Kerti herd ducks, there were two spoiled and pretty youngsters who were about to be initiated into the throes of teenage sex under circumstances precociously perverted. She was called Wisti and he was called Tulu, and this is how they happened to become the parents of the evil Klinyar.

Wisti and Tulu had been inching closer to full sexual consummation for some months. Wisti thought that by dangling her virginity in front of Tulu, keeping it just beyond his possession, she would surely win his true love forever. At first Tulu pursued Wisti's virginity almost idly, then with increasing covetousness, as if this were the most wonderful bauble on earth.

Each applied the best of their immature arts to the contest. Wisti bleached her face and redesigned her eyebrows and cultivated a rather original lisp. Tulu nurtured long fingernails on his left hand, perfumed his hair with the scented leaves of the *delem* plant, and developed a way of smoking that he thought made him look ruthless. Each spent much of the day in front of a mirror and could be coaxed into helping with the household chores by only the sweetest entreaties of their parents.

Every evening for months they had contrived to walk past each other, back and forth, each surrounded by a little claque of followers. Eventually Tulu would sprawl with his friends on the steps of the community pavilion, smoking cigarettes and perhaps pretending to be absorbed in the dandling of a fighting cock. Wisti and her friends, whom she selected carefully for their spotty skins and stubby bodies, would continue to stroll back and forth — pinching one another as they passed the boys, pretending to trip, feigning terminal coughs and whatever else they could think of to attract attention. The boys would blow smoke and belch and yell out things they thought to be killingly funny. Then one of the boys (never Tulu) would say something so outrageous that one of the girls (never Wisti) would have to go over to him and punch his arm, drawing the whole gaggle of girls with her. Before long the girls would settle on the steps a short distance from the boys — girls draped over girls, boys draped over boys, with both sides involved in a great deal of noisy display, jumping up, sitting down in a slightly more advantageous position, bumping into each other with little yelps, setting themselves up for more teasing, arm punching, wrist grabbing, and general showing off, until the two groups were more or less one group of teenagers and Wisti and Tulu were jostled into proximity. Then Wisti would arch her perfect ivory face for the private gaze of Tulu, and Tulu would toss his head and ensnare Wisti with the scent of his hair.

Then perhaps Tulu would complain of a headache and tell Wisti to massage his neck, and she would slap his arm and tell one of her minions — the thickest and spottiest — to massage it. The moment the poor spotty girl touched him, he'd yell out and Wisti would shove the girl away, muttering how stupid she was, and then place her own hands on the handsome shoulders of Tulu. She'd find herself startled by the sensation of touching him — a curling at the base of her spine, and her lips making a silent and involuntary movement: *mwah*.

As for Tulu, he was tortured by erections as painful as having a bone caught in his throat. He was forced to find relief for himself as quickly and privately and often as possible, but the relief never lasted, and within a few hours his eyes were aching in a headache that Wisti could do little to alleviate.

As time went on, Wisti and Tulu found it more and more difficult to disguise their lust and would think up increasingly flimsy pretexts to sneak off into the uncertain secrecy of a grove or the shadow of a palace wall, where they would sniff and pet each other, and moan and argue.

"Open your sarong," Tulu would beg.

"No, are you crazy?" Wisti would whisper, pressing herself against Tulu's hips with judicious accuracy. "Anyone could come along."

"Hold me," he'd say, directing her hand, "just for a minute. You don't love me, you don't know what a headache is like!" And he'd flex his beautiful nape.

"Is this your headache, down here?"

"Please … Oh. You make me feel so good."

Wisti also suffered from frustrated lust, but she had a more practical grasp of things. Privately, she had already decided to capitulate — to favor Tulu with the gift of her virginity — but she wanted her surrender to have maximum effect: Tulu must follow up with all the consequent honors. Several of Wisti's homelier friends had recently been swept off into the adult ranks of pregnancy and marriage, and she was disgusted by their sudden increase in prestige.

It was time to apply a bit of science, so she began to talk to her lover like this: "Tulu, my sweet love, I want to lie down with you!"

"Let's lie down! Take off your blouse."

"No, no, my darling, not like this. Slowly, in private. So I can see you. So you can see me."

Tulu was not about to strip naked ten feet from Wisti's front gate. He said, "Where? Where will we do it?"

"The graveyard," she said.

"The graveyard … let's go," he groaned.

"Not now. We have to plan this." She slipped her hand through the folds of his sarong. "Now listen. On Tilem we'll meet at the graveyard. And I'll let you do anything you want with me." (Tilem was the dark of the moon.)

"Oh, how can I see you on Tilem? Let's do it on Purnama. Let's do it in the moonlight." Purnama, the full moon, was six days away; Tilem twenty-one.

"No, no, no," said Wisti. This did not fit her calculations. "Tilem. At the graveyard." She had given considerable thought to her strategy. "We'll each carry three sticks of lighted incense, so we can find each other. And if anyone asks why we're carrying three sticks of incense, we can say because it's Tilem." Then she put her mouth over his, and with a few deft flicks of her wrist she consoled her lover and skipped up the steps of her front gate. The lamplight caught her jewelry, and sensing this she stopped, turned, and said to him, "And we won't speak again until then. This is our secret." Then, in the manner of an actress making her exit, she turned and slipped through the gate, into the dark.

So they disappeared into vestal retreat, and each began a program of assiduous narcissism. Wisti undertook to eat nothing but mangosteens, with the intention of making her flesh as delicious as that perfect fruit. Tulu required of his mother and sisters that he have the meat of a male animal every day, which caused them no little expense and considerable fibbing. The lovers forsook their evening promenade and aggravated the discomfort of their voluntary separation by the stealthy irritation of their genitals: in the case of Wisti, by the use of pastes of ginger and chillies and by carrying a small river stone in her rectum; in the case of Tulu, by the mere device of a ferocious asceticism.

During this period, the tempers of the two teenagers were infernal. Their families remarked among themselves how sullen their darlings had become, and noticed with distress the voraciousness of their shopping, the maniacal zeal of their grooming, and the cruelty they showed to the old people and caged birds in their house compounds.

At last the morning of the appointed Tilem arrived. Wisti prepared herself by remaining rigid on her cot, but this caused such alarm in the household that by midday she got up and apologized to everyone for having inconvenienced them, saying it was because she'd been trying to work out the design for a new necklace. She then left to gather leaves for a brew to restore her freshness. Tulu simply slipped off at dawn and spent a good part of the day cooling his hips in the river and working a concoction of flowers through his hair.

Dusk was never slower in coming. In their respective households, Wisti and Tulu made conspicuous displays of going to bed early. Their mothers had not yet finished ministering the offerings for Tilem when the sly children yawned grandly and bid their grandparents good night. After counting two hundred slow exhalations in the dark, they each slipped quietly out of their houses, taking care to steal three sticks of incense, and made their ardent ways to the graveyard.

O bridal night! O cinnamon! O soft darkness and coy footfall. O my perfumes, my personal sky! O thick, black colorless night with rocks and roots grabbing at my feet — O damned dark pig night! Wisti's right high-heeled sandal wobbled, and the earth slammed up and smacked her knee, elbow, chin. For a moment she lay frozen in disarray, senseless with outrage. Then, as the darkness grew tall above her, and her knee and elbow and chin began to swell with pain, she felt a whimper quivering within her, felt her nostrils pushing down toward her upper lip, and her lower lip arching up toward her nose. But just as her lips were about to break apart and give tongue to a real teen tantrum, she told herself: Stop it. Get up. This is your night.

Her three sticks of incense were still glowing. She waggled them experimentally, picked herself up, and steered herself magnetically toward the graveyard.

It was so dark that Wisti hardly knew if her eyes were open or closed. But her ears seemed to stretch, and all about her was a confusion of mutterings and rustlings. She smelled the meats and perfumes of offerings — and then she tripped again over someone sitting on the ground.

"Yeeesh," said Wisti.

"Yeeesh," said a woman (or a man) in the dark.

Wisti picked her way, almost crawling, in the directionless night. Here and there were pinpoints of incense, sometimes one, sometimes as many as five. She groped her way to a constellation of three.

"Is that you?"

"It's me, it's me," hissed Tulu.

"Oh, thank God. You wouldn't believe who else I've run into here tonight."

"Of course," said Tulu. "It's a good night for black magic."

"Shh!"

"Come here, I want to put some magic on you. Feel this."

"Stop that. Not here — anybody could come along," she said automatically.

"I'm feeling very magical," said Tulu.

"Don't. Oh! Oh, you smell wonderful."

"Who's that?"

Someone slammed into the lovers, a woman smelling of poultry.

"Tulu, let's get out of here."

"Over here. I know where we can go."

They made their way to the eastern edge of the graveyard and came to the Pura Dalem, the temple of the netherworld. Feeling their way with their hands, they slid along the wall and slipped in through the gate.

Inside the temple forecourt, they were alone. They could just make out the wide courtyard under the starry sky, and they instinctively crouched as if hiding from the eyes of the gods. The temple shrines and pavilions stood black against the sky. Wisti and Tulu clung to each other, hearts banging in panic and longing. Suddenly Tulu pinned Wisti against the base of the temple wall.

"Tulu, are you crazy? We can't do it in here. We could die!"

"I don't care. I love you so much, I'll die if you don't let me fuck you now. Oh, I feel sick, please, Wisti. It's now. Now!"

And it was done.

They lay for some time, sinking and floating in the realization that they had committed a crime of the most dangerous degree of sacrilege.

"We'll be put to death, Tulu. Together. The temple will have to be destroyed."

"Let's kill ourselves!"

"Yes! And we'll save the temple. Kill me first!" said Wisti, kissing Tulu's mouth over and over.

"Oh, yes!" said Tulu, heating to the idea. "I'll stab you first and then I'll kill myself. And then we'll be cremated together. Just like this."

Their awful destiny moved through them, filling their limbs, electrifying their skin.

"Wisti, before we die, let me see you naked."

"Not here. Not outdoors."

Together they got up and walked wordlessly, like condemned people, to the closed shrine that housed the holy dragon effigy, the Barong, where he rested in wide-eyed celestial sleep.

"It's locked," said Wisti.

"Of course it's locked," said Tulu, and he yanked the little padlock from the door. "Now come in."

Inside, they lit a tiny oil lamp and saw looming above them the huge accoutrements of the Barong. The holy harness of gilded leather, goat hair, crow feathers, tiny mirrors, and human hair spanned nearly fifteen feet. It hung from the rafters so that no part of it came in contact with the floor. The mask itself, the holiest part of all, was shrouded with a piece of white cloth. Wisti, with a drunken smile on her face, plucked off the cloth and sat back before the Barong's unblinking and ecstatic stare. Slowly, humming a hymn she had known all her life, she untied her sarong.

The sin that followed was unspeakable. It went on for hours, until the chill before dawn when finally the lovers were glutted and sour. Tulu tossed Wisti's sarong limply at her. "This is unbelievable," he said. "Now I'll really have to kill myself."

"Shut up. Put the cloth back on the … you know, and let's go home. Lock up carefully. It was amazing. We just won't do it again." Then she added, "Tulu, it was … I think we've done something like … Well, you have to marry me now."

And thus the soul of Ni Klinyar burst into the dimension of life-on-earth, conceived in sin and signified by a secret climate of curse.

Some weeks later, Tulu and Wisti were holding lengths of cloth against themselves before the mirror in Wisti's room. The door was half open, to keep little children from becoming curious and looking in. Wisti arched her face to catch the light.

"I think I'm late," she said. "Move a little, will you? I can't see anything."

O<small>N GUNUNG KAWI</small>, the land seemed to stand in the sky. Fog and sunlight moved through the forest and over the farms of Mpu Dibiaja, breeding mosses and tall scented trees and billowing clouds of birdsong. Wild roses ranged over fields of grass, and bees swarmed in the rain forest. In this high country of timber and orchids and wild beasts, an ancient and pristine magic still lived — in the rocks and valleys and rivers, in monstrous trees and tiny undiscovered flowers, and in everything that lived and grew there — and the honey, too, from Gunung Kawi was said to have magical properties.

Siladri stayed on at the house of Mpu Dibiaja. First there were the long, complicated rituals to dispel the death of Kadek and erase all traces of her physical form from the world. For Siladri, this time passed like dreaming, strange with the murmuring of animals. Then there was a very long time when Siladri seemed to have no thoughts at all, but wandered for hours in the forests and fields of Gunung Kawi. Often Mpu Dibiaja found him sitting on a hillside with Kusuma Sari, weaving grasses into a necklace or simply watching her as she lay in the sun with the lioness.

Mpu Dibiaja's house was large and comfortable, composed of broad courtyards and finely made pavilions. There were kitchens and granaries and places to read, and a number of different places to sleep, for there were often guests: pilgrims; disciples; and people who came to ask help of Mpu Dibiaja, sometimes people like Siladri and Kusuma Sari, who fell out of the sky at his doorstep and were in fact mendicants.

The courtyards were clean-swept spaces with planted intervals of flowering trees and vines (for there was sensuousness, too, in celibacy): frangipani, ylang-ylang, hibiscus, passion fruit, roses, the velvety *mussaenda*, and the creeping, night-flowering jasmine. Here the ghostly *nagasari* tree was robust and silvery and flexible, like a young swordsman; and there were big, sticky blossoms that filled Siladri with a puzzling melancholy.

There were rich vegetable gardens and high fields of hard red mountain rice. All around grew wild marigolds, bursts of lemon grass, sturdy bushes of native spinach, and free-ranging wild tomatoes, small and savory and smelling of pepper.

The science of Mpu Dibiaja's gardening was so subtle that it was never clear where his gardens ended and the forest began, for in the forest, too, was evidence of the old man's nurturing: beehives and deep stands of ground orchids and groves of cinnamon and coffee and oranges and cloves. There were lime trees and cashew trees and tall trees of avocado, jackfruit, mango, and mangosteen. Siladri learned to find the wild bitter lettuces that Mpu Dibiaja loved, and in the warm rainy nights of winter, he gathered secretive mushrooms to offer his patron.

One day some months after the cremation of his wife, Siladri approached the pavilion where Mpu Dibiaja was transcribing a manuscript. Siladri sat down before him on the ground.

"Mpu Dibiaja, several months ago I came to your house, a stranger with a dead woman and a motherless infant. I could hardly have been a greater imposition —"

Mpu Dibiaja burst out laughing and looked at Siladri. "I've had more troublesome visitors than you, my dear. Get up."

Siladri carried on with what he had prepared to say. "And yet you've done so much to help us. You've given us shelter and kindness and guidance. I'm ashamed to even speak of how greatly I'm indebted to you. You have rescued us." Here he stopped and bit his lips together. Mpu Dibiaja interrupted.

"Siladri, it's good of you to say those things. But, you know, you are not indebted to us. On the contrary, you have given us the pleasure of having been of help. You are quite free to go and never think of us again."

Siladri clasped his hands under his chin and fixed his eyes on those of his rescuer. "Please, no! Mpu Dibiaja, if I am free to go, may I perhaps also be allowed to stay and offer you my labor? Surely there's some way I could be useful here. Perhaps fetching water or helping to dig the gardens. Please! There's nothing I wouldn't be grateful to do, if only I may stay." He realized that he was begging, and thought: Yes, in fact I am begging. "I'm also thinking of Kusuma Sari," he said. "She's so happy and healthy here, and —"

"And such a lovely baby," said Mpu Dibiaja. "Yes, please do stay with us as long as you like. The child needs a mother, and here she has several."

Siladri now came to the part he dreaded telling, the spiny knowledge he'd carried in his heart from the first night he spent at Mpu Dibiaja's house. He would pull it out now.

"Sir, I must tell you something about us." He told the whole story of his decision to leave his village and of the exchange of children with Madé Kerti, all up until his arrival at Gunung Kawi. "So you see," he concluded, "she does have parents and a home. I confess, I don't know what to do. I should take her back, but she's, well, you know her. And she's all I have to love. Oh, I love you greatly, you must know that, but my arms would be so empty without Kusuma Sari." Siladri covered his face with his hands and began to cry there on the ground.

"Of course, Siladri, of course. That's why she's with you. Accept Kusuma Sari — she's a gift from your brother. And accept your welcome here. You are as much as ever like my own son. Think of this house as yours. You are free to do whatever you like. Stay! Of course you may help out, if that appeals to your fancy. Or stay in bed all day, it's perfectly all right, my dear. Now why are you crying again?"

For several years Siladri thought of nothing but the gardens and the unfolding enchantment of his daughter.

By his own choice they slept on the kitchen bed, nestled between the lioness and the doe. Sometimes in the evenings on his way to the kitchen with Kusuma Sari, he passed the pavilion where Mpu Dibiaja sat in the lamplight with his books, muttering scripture. Siladri would just smile; the vanity of his spiritual ambitions, which had cost the life of Kadek, filled him with such shame that his heart was empty of books.

But the time came when Siladri could no longer ignore the fact of books. Kusuma Sari had begun to draw in the dirt, and one day she drew a perfect syllable. Siladri whisked her up in his arms and said, "Ooh, my little bird, not on the ground! The alphabet belongs to Sang Hyang Aji Saraswati. Writing is holy." He brought her directly to the master's pavilion and set her before what people used in those days for pen and paper: fine dried leaves, a sharpened bamboo stick, and indigo ink.

Holding her on his lap, Siladri showed her. "Like this. Oh, what a clever girl." Man and child sat as one body and together they slowly drew the alphabet. The afternoon light warmed around them, sinking into gold.

Mpu Dibiaja found them there at dusk as he came in from the flower garden. He held a tiger cub in his arms, and a swarm of fireflies floated around his head. The old man stopped and watched Siladri and Kusuma Sari bent over their work. Siladri drew the letters, pronouncing them slowly while Kusuma Sari's hand rested on his and her voice curled high inside the voice of her father.

"So our little girl is teaching you the alphabet," said Mpu Dibiaja, and he gave them a wonderful smile, oblivious to the fireflies blinking in his hair.

The next night Siladri sat with Mpu Dibiaja on the same pavilion, with Kusuma Sari asleep on his lap. A little lamp burned on the table between them. It was Purnama, the full moon, and offerings had been placed, fragrant and lovely, around the key points of the house, filling the air with the sweet nostalgia of incense.

They had been chatting all evening — about trees and rain, and principles of architecture, and the divine provenance of writing — when suddenly Mpu Dibiaja took Siladri's hand and said, "I will die before you two. You shall be my heir, Siladri. Now what?"

Siladri looked at the old magician. He looked around at the house and courtyards, and he listened to the night air and the sound of the child's breathing and the breathing of the sleeping pilgrims, and of the animals asleep in the kitchen and in the doorways and far away in the forest, and he said, "How could I possibly take your place?"

Mpu Dibiaja looked at Siladri and said nothing.

Siladri said, "Teach me what I need to know."

The old man smiled and sighed. His smile grew wider and brighter in the lamplight between them. "There now," said Mpu Dibiaja. "I thought you'd never ask."

Thus Siladri came at last to be the pupil of Mpu Dibiaja. Over the next seven years Mpu Dibiaja gathered and concentrated the full web of his knowledge and tinctured it to Siladri with all the patience of his wizardry.

Mpu Dibiaja was a renowned healer, and he encouraged Siladri to be present when he received the sick. He taught him how to examine the afflicted: to listen carefully to the person's seven pulses, to listen as well for the voices of the illness and chart its origin and meaning. He initiated Siladri into the names of the shifting humors of the body and soul, and drilled him in the genealogies of the divinities of healing. He taught him mantras and recipes of exorcism, powerful workings of prayer by which the pathogen is invoked — how it is summoned, honored with descriptions, and invited to accept an alternate offering and leave the sick person to recover his health in peace.

Mpu Dibiaja taught Siladri the language through which he communicated with the animals and instructed him in the protocol of their ways.

He taught him many other useful things: how to draw nourishment from the air, how to find sleep in the wakefulness of meditation, how to travel in the guise of a kingfisher or a glass of water. And always Kusuma Sari was present at these lessons.

Mpu Dibiaja taught Siladri the nature and practical uses of *sakti*, that charismatic instrument of the heart that is the faculty of magic. He made it clear from the beginning that *sakti* was wild and ambivalent and was present everywhere (like electricity and the nuclear mysteries, which they called by other names). *Sakti* was like weather, like passion, like …

"Like lightning at your private command, Siladri. *Sakti* is the most terrible and beautiful possibility available to mankind — a chance to behave on the same octave as nature. It is way over our heads, Siladri, and it would explode us where we sit if we did not contain it with the Dharma." The old man turned to Kusuma Sari. "Tell me, my little fairy, what is the Dharma?"

Kusuma Sari smiled into the face of Mpu Dibiaja and said, "I'm sorry, sir, I don't know."

"Ah, but you already do. The Dharma is living with love and respect toward everything and everyone."

Siladri was frozen for an instant by the thought of his brother Kerti, the plump practitioner of what is right and good.

The Dharma, explained Mpu Dibiaja, was a way of choosing. And it was the harmony latent in all things — heaven on earth — but it was also periodically forgotten; in Kali Yuga, men had to learn it again. Some people knew it without learning — again Siladri thought of Madé Kerti; others, like Siladri, chased it with their minds; some people were ascetics.

"Like you, my good teacher," said Siladri.

"Well, it hardly counts anymore. There's very little left for me to renounce, and existence itself is a pleasure, so what can you do?"

The Dharma was something to learn to long for, to develop a taste for. You could learn to perceive it if you could just become quiet enough, like an empty house with all its doors and windows wide open, and the Dharma would move through you like a warm scented wind.

"You must understand," continued Mpu Dibiaja, "that *sakti* is abroad in the world for anyone to master, and there are those who by conscious manipulation of the Dharma — and this is an ugly thing, Siladri, but true, and I think you may have to see it firsthand one day — there are those who can accomplish quite horrible sorts of miracles."

"Witches?" said Siladri.

"My dear Siladri, I too am a witch. It's quite the same issue. There is only one God and only one Science. This should already be obvious. A witch's enemy is utterly intimate: it is oneself. The key is to give oneself over entirely to the Dharma. For the Dharma is hugely sacred. Its origin is divine. No human being could have conjured it — it treats of perfection itself in the human sphere, and nowhere else is perfection so elusive as in the human sphere."

Siladri listened.

Mpu Dibiaja continued, giving Siladri the betelnut box. "The interesting thing about being a human being is that one may choose *not* to live by the Dharma."

"But why would one not?" said Siladri.

"Oh, goodness, there are fortunes to be made by running *sakti* counter to the Dharma. Think of what it means: extraordinary powers put to the service of desire or greed or anger. In Kali Yuga, only eccentrics try to unite *sakti* to the Dharma. I suppose you already know that we are eccentric?"

At this, Mpu Dibiaja gave a tiny smile that reminded Siladri of Ni Sabuk. Am I getting homesick? Siladri wondered.

"Your prayers can bring you grace or poison," said Mpu Dibiaja. "So pray always for grace."

But Siladri was cursed with a volatile mind, and he felt he could find no peace until he understood the entire architecture of the human soul.

One night Siladri asked Mpu Dibiaja if there was ever an instance when one must break with the Dharma.

"Of course not. The Dharma contains everything," said Mpu Dibiaja.

"Let me propose a hypothetical example," said Siladri. "According to the Dharma, it is wrong to steal, isn't that so?"

"That is so," said Mpu Dibiaja.

"Suppose there is an earthquake and the rice fields are destroyed. And the farmers' houses are destroyed, too, and the farmers have no place to live and nothing to eat. And let's say that the king has granaries, perhaps in another part of the country, that have not been destroyed, and the farmers go there and take the king's grain. Are they criminals?"

"Yes, they're criminals. It's against the law."

"But an unjust law," said Siladri.

"It's against the Dharma to steal."

"I suppose," said Siladri, "that a saint would decline to steal. He'd rather die."

"Of course he would. So what?"

"Suppose the saint had a hungry child," said Siladri. "Would the saint oblige his child to die of starvation with him?"

"The saint would probably forego his saintliness and become a criminal to feed his child." Mpu Dibiaja laughed loud and long at this.

"But would the person who steals to feed a child be judged as harshly as the person who steals for greed?"

"That's not for us to know, my dear. Now don't make such a face. The Dharma is the law that says *sakti* — and all the rest of nature — always brings about its proper consequences. The law also says that we must be kind to each other, that we must live within the ritual order of our sort, and that we may not break the rules of men without being subject to their punishment. Now what's the problem?"

"And what is heaven?"

"Another time, Siladri. You asked me about criminals. To live in contradiction to the law is to be a criminal. Do we understand each other so far?"

"Yes."

"Then you must remember to have pity on criminals, because they will surely suffer greatly for their sins. And if you yourself must one day commit a crime, don't worry, my scrupulous friend — you will be punished."

The two men sat for a while without saying anything. As always when they spoke at night, Kusuma Sari slumbered in the arms of Siladri, warmed by the hum of speech coming from his body. Finally Siladri said to Mpu Dibiaja, "I can't help wondering what kind of future you are preparing me for."

"I'm sorry that I cannot tell you what your future holds."

"But do you know what my future holds?" Siladri realized that this sort of question was contrary to the etiquette of speaking with sorcerers; it was a question about the sorcerer's own powers — but he couldn't help it.

"I know a little about what things may come your way," Mpu Dibiaja said. "But I cannot know how you'll react to them. In that sense, the future hasn't happened yet. Let us think instead about who we are now, and what we know of things as they are. This is what matters."

One evening, some years earlier, when Kusuma Sari was about four and already old enough to start learning to make offerings, Siladri and his teacher had a remarkable conversation.

"My children," said Mpu Dibiaja, "I am an old man, and you must permit me to tell you what I have discovered. First and last in human life is *rahayu* — that is, gratefulness for things as they are. There is nothing else to know."

Siladri said, "Nothing else to know? Then how do we not know it? And how is it that there seem to be so many other things to learn as well?"

"Now that is the interesting part about life-on-earth," said Mpu Dibiaja. He turned to Kusuma Sari. "Sari, that is very pretty. I think I have never seen a finer maker of offerings than you. But let me show you a little detail ... There, now you have it."

"Just so!" said Siladri. "If all we need to know is to be happy with things as they are, why do we work to perfect our skills in the world? If the truth is, as the holy books say, that we are entirely God, then —"

"But, my dear," said Mpu Dibiaja, "just look at us."

Siladri felt exasperated. "Yes, indeed. Look at us! Life seems to me to be very complicated. Even the science of life is complicated. And humankind is so very, very complicated."

"So it is," said Mpu Dibiaja. "We have often remarked this."

Siladri stared at his teacher and then dropped his head.

"Well? Go on," said Mpu Dibiaja.

"I don't know how to go forward. I've come to you to find some stream of perfection in existence. To learn to know God and to live a life of goodness. And still I understand nothing, and my soul feels like broken bones. Nothing has changed except that my poor wife died of exhaustion — of obedience to a selfish husband. I sit at the feet of the wisest, kindest man on earth, and everything he tells me turns to riddles." Siladri sat up sharply and then bent toward his teacher. "Gratefulness for things as they are! *Rahayu*! Where shall I find this *rahayu*?"

Mpu Dibiaja stared at Siladri and blinked a little, and then he said, "There is nothing to find. It's already with you. It's been with you forever and ever, and you can't even be rid of it. You could throw yourself into the sea a thousand times and you would still finally be nothing but perfect love. This is a fact, Siladri."

Siladri rubbed his hands over his face and then began to roll himself a cigarette. His head and chest were beating hard. He lit the cigarette from their lamp and smoked for a while, hoping to calm down. "You must find me very stupid," he said. "I find myself very stupid. All existence, you say, is love ... is God. That is very beautiful.

And yet you admit that we are all nonetheless clumsy, in varying degrees. You are a healer: that presupposes disease. If all existence is God, why is there sickness and stupidity? You answer me that that is what is 'interesting' about human life. Now I beg you, tell me what this human life is. Tell me why there is pain and fear. Tell me why we see people here every day with misshapen bones, and fevers that make them believe they are monkeys and goats, and wounds inflicted by their own brothers and aunts? Why are farmers beaten and robbed by their princes? Why does a simple girl die under a tree before she's ever seen her own son walk toward her? Why is it that the more a man prays, the more he hears no other voice than his own?" The cigarette between Siladri's fingers had become dangerously short. Mpu Dibiaja leaned over and plucked it from his pupil's hand. "Tell me, teacher, why these things are!" And then: "Forgive me if I shout. I do not shout at you. But I am your very stupid disciple, and I am asking for help."

Mpu Dibiaja took a short puff on the stub of the cigarette he had taken from Siladri and tossed it away. Then he said, "Come here, my dear, and sit beside me. You remind me of much that I had forgotten. Do come and sit next to me." Siladri moved closer to his teacher. "I have asked you to be my son, this is true. And it is fair that you ask me to tell you these things — very like a son, and I thank you. You always make me happy. But what could I tell you, Siladri, that you would believe? That wonderful mind of yours is like an angry snake. It will be a marvelous instrument one day. But one day you will die and your mind will die. So you see, it's not all that wonderful. Let's warm it with your heart."

Siladri did not know what to say. He picked up Kusuma Sari, who was dozing against his side, and put her in his lap.

Mpu Dibiaja continued. "Why do you think we sing our books? Conversations are very good, Siladri. I like talking with you in the evening like this. But I want to propose an exercise for you. When you have a question, would you please sing it?"

Siladri opened his mouth to answer, and Mpu Dibiaja raised his forefinger. Siladri held his reply inside himself and let it steep for a moment as he searched for an appropriate meter. A little smile flickered between the man and the master, and then Siladri settled back and sang:

Where is my place in this world?
Whom do I ask, and who is singing?

The song lifted out over the rooftops of Mpu Dibiaja's house and took the shape of a blue wolf. It had a long bushy tail and its head was set at an angle that bent toward the sky. Siladri and Mpu Dibiaja watched the wolf float out over the mountain, following the direction of its jaws. Its contours soon became tattered and vague, like clouds do when they are on the march, and before long the shape was lost among the mists of the night sky.

"That was very good," said Mpu Dibiaja, and he sat back, eyes wide. "What else?"

"Angels!" sang Siladri unexpectedly.

Angels singing through me,
Sing through me! Sing through me!
Take me! Take me for your music,
Make music of my singing, Angels!

This song rose in a soaring of gold and burst into a many-headed bouquet. Blossoms of unimaginable shapes fell away and fluttered down into the forest. Several of them were caught in the webs of night spiders. The spiders were eaten by larks in the morning, and in this way Siladri's song-blossoms became part of the language of the birds.

"My dear Siladri!" said Mpu Dibiaja, and the two of them laughed out loud. Kusuma Sari turned in her sleep and curled against her father. Siladri gathered her against his chest and he sank down again into his lake of song. For some time there was only the sound of their breathing and of the wind beyond the walls. And then Siladri began to sing again, but softly now:

Little traveler, like a lily
Pond, faceless in space, sleeping
And smiling, you are
Like a lily in my arms,
Like a leaf upon a lake.
Little visitor, how perfect you are.

Sleep, my little night flower,
I will watch over you; my love
Will protect you, and tomorrow
My love will show you the way home.

The music seeped through their clothes and into the memories of Siladri and Mpu Dibiaja and Kusuma Sari. Then everything was very quiet, and Mpu Dibiaja and Siladri could hear a little snore coming from Kusuma Sari. Siladri sang again, but this time his song did not reach his lips. It remained deep within his heart, sounding like this:

Child of God, gift from heaven,
Rest with me a little longer.
Let me be your lamp, little candle.
Let our light be brave and bright,
And let us be a signal in the dark,
And let us wait together in the night.

And then, "Bless us. God bless us. May God bless us."

As she grew, Kusuma Sari became an observer and then a helper in the nurturing work of Mpu Dibiaja's household, and she showed an unusual aptitude for the magical arts.

Because of her early intimacy with the animals, she excelled her father in conversation with them: Siladri's puns were never very successful, and his language with Sang-Gadja-the-Elephant was almost comically formal. But both Siladri and Kusuma Sari came to master the languages of the birds, and learned to hear, in their speech, news of lands distant and near.

Kusuma Sari, they found, had a gift for healing. Whereas Siladri was soon a brilliant diagnostician (and not only by his intellectual power: he was cursed with the rare and uncomfortable ability to feel a person's illness as his own, and in the early years of his practice his sympathy often caused him to cry out alongside his patients), it was Kusuma Sari whose firm little hands and sweet words comforted the sick and quieted their fears.

The education of Kusuma Sari was not all wizardry and books. She also learned the simpler things that women need to know: how to build a fire and make it leap or purr; she learned to swirl the raw rice on a flat round tray of woven bamboo and to toss the grains in the air so that the wind took away the dust; she learned how to climb like a goat up from the river gorge with a jug of sloshing water on her head, finding toeholds in the tree roots.

Kusuma Sari learned to scrub their clothes in the river with fine sand and soap nuts, and to bleach cloth in the antiseptic light of the sun. She learned to make mats from the dried leaves of the pandanus, and to roast coffee so that it was as rich as chocolate. Most important, she learned to make the vast vocabulary of offerings that were essential to life as a human being.

Who taught the work of women to Kusuma Sari? It was Mpu Dibiaja, who knew all the labor of men and women. He taught Kusuma Sari to prepare the daily sambal, which was the cornerstone of a man's happiness in eating rice: a handful of little red chillies, tiny onions, and plump garlic; the concocted medicine that is shrimp paste; rough crunchy sea salt; oil that has been coaxed from the coconut; the crisp perfumes of lemon grass and the waxy, aromatic *kecicang* flower; all of this pounded together with tender green peppercorns and, sometimes, the smoked twists of roasted baby eels (for in Bali in those days, people were frank about life and death, and they ate meat gratefully, with an intimate knowledge of where it came from).

On Gunung Kawi, as most everywhere in Bali, people ate in privacy — that is, by turning their backs — the better to savor the day's meal: a banana leaf of hot rice punctuated by the serial surprises of condiments — salty, rich, pungent, fiery, fragrant — all given crunch by roasted groundnuts, and afterwards a cleansing rinse of one's fingers, teeth, and gums with hot water flavored with ginger root.

Kusuma Sari also learned to supervise the poultry yard, selecting the hens for breeding and the chicks, by their colors, for later ritual use. With a breeder's eye, she learned to choose the roosters: each was given a season's training in combat by the men of the household; a stable of cocks was maintained for ritual cockfights. If a cock won three times, Kusuma Sari decreed, he had earned retirement; then he could run among the hens in the garden, in the unrestrained pursuit of love.

In the same spirit, Kusuma Sari nurtured the piglets. She cooked up great pots of soup for them, bathed them daily, and massaged them when they were rheumatic in the rainy season — until they became huge and grave and ready for sacrifice at the rich festival of Galungan.

As Kusuma Sari grew, her eyes became attuned to the life of the garden. She could read the complexions of the leaves and take the pulse of the soil. She was always the first to see the blurt of orange in a papaya tree; she delighted in the big brown lines of a ripening banana tree as it sent all its force through its trunk into the display of fruit at its terminus; and she was happiest of all on that day, twice a year, when the coffee trees were in flower, turning the world white and drenching it with perfume.

Mpu Dibiaja taught Kusuma Sari the science of the market: how many eggs for how much salt; so many bushels of sweet corn for a bolt of cloth; a piglet for a plow and so many earthen pots; marigolds for sewing needles; and roses for shrimp paste and ink.

Under Mpu Dibiaja's tutelage, Kusuma Sari learned that farming was the management of life and death. She knew that life's richest food is death, and understood the usefulness of discarded things: the peels of a mound of garlic, the carcass of a hummingbird, the wastes of the stable and of expired offerings. Such things she put back into the earth with the same cheer as that with which she cut down the ripe baggage of bananas or bid permission from a tree to harvest its flowers.

Kusuma Sari learned early to appreciate the ingenuity of nature. One day when she was about six years old, she witnessed the birth of two deer, and she remarked on the economy of nature that provides a restorative meal for the dam in the form of the afterbirth. Kusuma Sari spoke of it that evening to Mpu Dibiaja and Siladri.

"Mémé-the-Deer had two chicks today."

"Calves," corrected Siladri.

"Your little sisters," added Mpu Dibiaja, who had already called on the dam.

"And Mémé cried while they were being born. She called out for her mother and then for her husband, and then Mémé's bottom pointed up to the trees like she was sick, and then my sisters came out like slippery blue poop, first one and then the second one, then do you know what happened?"

"Tell us, darling," said Siladri.

"Then Mémé began to eat the blue skin of my sisters, and she was hiccupping a little, and then, then there was … there was this blue thing like an egg, but with no shell."

"That's a very fine observation," said Siladri, graying.

"That was the afterbirth," said Mpu Dibiaja, "Raja Banaspati, the lord of the forest. A most wonderful thing!"

"And then Mémé sniffed this afterforth —"

"After*birth*."

"Afterbirth. And she said so many things and called out so many names — and some of the names she gave to my first sister and then she gave some names to my second sister, and then she ate the blue egg. She ate it! And then she stretched for a minute, very silky, and then she moved my sisters around with her nose and showed them where the milk is, but I just let them. I already have all the milk I need."

"What a big girl now to have two more little sisters," said Mpu Dibiaja.

"And was the husband there too?" said Siladri, tears rising inexplicably in his eyes.

Of all the things Kusuma Sari learned, she most loved the study of scripture. It was here that she and Siladri found their greatest harmony, and their delight in reading the holy poetry transported them beyond the virtuosity of even their old teacher.

One night when Kusuma Sari was about eleven years old, the three of them were sitting as usual in the reading pavilion. Siladri and Kusuma Sari were reading aloud together. Mpu Dibiaja had long ceased to take part, preferring instead to listen and admire. He had become very old and his eyes could see only distant things clearly. For the past weeks he had asked Siladri and Kusuma Sari to read from the *Adiparwa* about the world beyond the world. Siladri knew this text to be especially beloved among old people, but he was surprised when Mpu Dibiaja said at the end of their chapter, "Yes, indeed. Let us read until morning."

When morning finally came and the sun was touching the highest points of the trees, Mpu Dibiaja said, "Thank you, my children. That was very beautiful. Now bid me good morning and goodbye."

Siladri and Kusuma Sari felt the songs drain from their bodies. They saw a white light, brighter even than the sunlight, radiating from their teacher. Kusuma Sari began to cry and she reached out toward Mpu Dibiaja, but Siladri stayed her hands. They watched as their patron slowly disappeared before their eyes. Soon there was nothing but a bright cloud in front of them. By the time the sun had reached its zenith, the radiance had shrunk to a tiny gleam, and then it lifted and floated away into the white of the sky.

N<small>I</small> K<small>LINYAR</small>, now the six-year-old daughter of Wisti and Tulu, was a queer-looking little girl, subject to violent changes of color — sometimes entirely lavender, sometimes entirely lime green, even to her eyelashes. When she was in a bad temper, she seemed to pulsate in repugnant switches of burnt orange and chocolate bog. It was during these last color spells that she was inclined to kill things, such as big, sleepy spiders and butterflies, but also plants in flower, and kittens. Once her mother found her in a tangerine rage, with nothing else to injure than half a dozen freshly gathered eggs, which she was methodically pressing against the kitchen wall, slowly, as if to savor the crushing of the shell and the luminescent ooze of life lost.

Her parents were naturally frightened of her. They did not allow her to leave the house compound — but of course she often did anyway, and her infamy quickly spread.

As to the profanity in which Klinyar was conceived, her parents never confessed it to anyone. The temple itself did not have to be burned after all: a natural disaster all but destroyed it not long after that noxious copulation, when the ancient and gigantic banyan tree outside its gates lifted in its roots and hurled itself down on the temple, scattering the stones of the walls, tearing down shrines with its branches, and crushing under its great trunk several important pavilions — the *balé gong* where the instruments of the gamelan orchestra were stored, the kitchens, and the pavilion of the Barong, the holy dragon.

The entire community was stunned. A wave of panic raced

through the village as people wondered what disgrace could have caused such a calamity.

"It was all that witchcraft going on in the graveyard."

"It was a windy night and the tree was already old."

"There was no wind that night!"

"The gods were unhappy with their offerings during the last temple festival. I told you we shouldn't have used palm leaves from outside the village."

"Oh, it wasn't the palm leaves. It was those cheap ducks from over the river. Who *knows* where they'd been eating."

"Well, someone desecrated the temple, it's obvious."

"Maybe there's a corpse buried there."

"The gate was in the wrong place. I've always thought so."

And so forth.

Everyone in the village who had been guilty of magical ill will — and there were many — called for drastic measures.

The village council met and decided to invoke the gods to speak of their anger and prescribe what must be done to restore their favor.

For the next several months, a series of trance rituals took place, over which time the village gathered detailed instructions from the gods for the building of the new temple and the ceremonies to be held at various stages of construction. A new Barong was ordered; the battered remains of the original were commanded to be cremated.

The rebuilding of the temple took four years and cost the people heavily in labor and materials. The village voted onerous taxes on themselves, and the families of Wisti and Tulu were surprised by the willingness of the young newlyweds to donate their jewelry. "Marriage has made them responsible," they concluded.

For, as Wisti had planned, Tulu married her as soon as it was clear that she would bear this misbegotten child. For a while, though, Wisti's future as a wife and mother had been uncertain.

"Don't have the baby, Wis'," urged Tulu. "It's bad luck."

"How can you talk like that? This is our love child — your son!"

"I think you'd enjoy learning to ride a motorbike, Wis'."

"You know, your hair smells funny. You should wash it more often."

The cruel nature of their little girl and her untoward ability to change hue made Wisti and Tulu worry that the destruction of the temple might be traced to their crime. More than one old hag had kept count of the dates and called Klinyar a hell child. Wisti and Tulu decided to look for professional help — that is, they sought out sorcerers.

In Bali at this time, there were witches who did well for themselves by exploiting the island's complex lore of magic. Wisti and Tulu would bring Klinyar to the house of a *balian*, someone with a reputation for solving problems through magical means. Wisti would bring a small offering and have tucked into her clothes a goodly sum of money, just in case.

The courtyard of the *balian*, where people waited, was often crowded, and everyone stole sly glances at everyone else, to see who had what. (Those looking for magical help usually went to someone far from their own village. It was important to be discreet.)

When their turn came, Wisti and Tulu would approach the pavilion where the *balian* sat. It might be a woman, but more often it was a man, and always his head was wrapped in a headcloth, and usually his fingernails were dirty.

"So what can I do for you?" the *balian* would say, looking carefully at the quality of the clothes and jewelry of his petitioners.

"It's our little girl," they would say, and then Wisti would recite their lament. "She's impossible, Jero Balian. She throws her food around, and bites her grandmother, and kicks over my toy-table. She takes off her clothes in the street and curses during prayers."

"Has she had all her childhood ceremonies?" the *balian* would ask.

"Of course she has," Wisti would say, always offended by the suggestion that her child was not ritually up-to-date. "But the worst is that she turns colors."

"Turns colors? What do you mean, madam?"

"She turns the most disgusting colors. It gives me such awful headaches, sometimes I have to lie down for the whole afternoon in a darkened room." Here Wisti would dab at her eyes with a little handkerchief.

"Let me examine her," the *balian* would say, and, like our own doctors, he would feel the little girl's glands and look at her eyes and tongue. And always Klinyar would be on her best behavior, as if she knew this made her parents peevish and discredited their stories.

"She turns colors, you say?"

"Yes, when she's in her tempers," Wisti would say. "Not that she'd be so kind as to oblige me now."

Then the *balian* would say, "Your child has been bewitched."

The next step would be to find out who caused the spell, and here there was a great variety of techniques. Sometimes the *balian* would put his hands around Klinyar's head and chant with his eyes rolled back white. Sometimes he would take their little offering over to a shrine, go into trance, and ask who was causing this evil. Sometimes the *balian* would smoke Klinyar with a bundle of incense sticks. Sometimes he'd blow sharply into her ear or pinch the tips of her fingers and toes, and throughout all this Klinyar would remain somber and sad and of perfectly ordinary coloring. But afterward — when the *balian* had sold the parents a little bottle of oil said to contain gold or in which, he said, a magical kris had been dipped — afterward, when they'd left the *balian*'s house and were back in the street, Klinyar would sink her teeth into her mother's hand and soil her underclothes.

For almost a year, Wisti and Tulu visited different *balian* — sometimes as often as five or six times, sometimes only once (as when the *balian* suggested that perhaps the problem was with the parents), but nearly always at considerable expense. They were exhorted to buy various spells that the *balian* would cast for a certain fee, and they were also urged to purchase magical belts, rings, drawings, liniments, and amulets containing bits of bone, skin, insect parts, venom, excreta, and many unidentifiable substances.

The ritual prescriptions were costly, and the harried young parents of Klinyar were quickly relieved of what was left of their jewelry.

They owned only a little land, and when that, too, was threatened, they found themselves one day in a different sort of negotiation.

"Your daughter has been bewitched," said yet another *balian*.

Wisti rolled her eyes.

"So we've been told," said Tulu.

"You say she turns colors?" said the *balian*.

They nodded.

"Perhaps she can be cured, but she would have to spend some time away from home," said the *balian*. He watched the mother's reaction carefully.

"Away from home?" said Wisti, brightening.

"Treatments," said the *balian*. "It could take quite some time. Possibly years."

"I want only what's best for my child," said Wisti.

"We're prepared to make sacrifices to ensure the best possible treatment for our little girl," said Tulu.

Klinyar growled softly and turned a pale turquoise.

The *balian* looked on. His face was still, and his eyes were bright slits. "Let me see if I can arrange it. Come back in fifteen days. Bring three gold coins and a young rooster with red, green, black, and white tail feathers. You may leave the gold coins now if you have them. I'll have to make a journey."

In the floating world of that particular kind of *balian*, there existed an inner hierarchy of sorcery — not precisely political, but rather orbits of admiration that gravitated toward an exclusive center. When Klinyar's parents thought about these events years later, they recalled that long before they'd noticed it, there had been an interest in Klinyar from some obscure but significant magical quarter. That interest emanated from the arch witch Dayu Datu.

A child with faculties of mutation and a bad temper could be molded into a formidable weapon. A deal was arranged.

The transaction, carried out through intermediaries and with all due account for protocol both calendric and personal, took forty-two days to negotiate. In intervals of three days, and five and seven, with adjustments for the progress of the moon and the decay of the season, it was gradually agreed that the child Ni Klinyar, aged eight, accompanied by four sacks of raw rice, a black rooster, three batik sarongs, two thousand Chinese coins, several loops of cotton string (black, red, and plain white), a young yellow coconut and various other implements of Balinese ritual, plus several more unusual items — a size 32AA brassiere, a bottle of nail polish remover, and a Japanese-Indonesian dictionary — for this bride gold, then, little Klinyar would be taken off the hands of her exhausted and embarrassed parents, although by exactly whom they never knew.

The goods were collected and assembled. On the morning of the appointed day, Klinyar's grandmother supervised the preparations for the girl's departure. The young mother had suddenly been overwhelmed with grief at the impending loss of her child, and she moved wanly about the house in a loose dress, with a paste of herbs on her forehead; her husband busied himself with a young rooster. Klinyar herself was unusually quiet.

At last they set off, parents, child, grandmother, bearers, and one or two hangers-on who dropped behind at the edge of the village. At some distance farther, they came to the crossroads specified in their instructions.

"Now, Klinyar," said her grandmother, "you wait right here and someone will come for you. Don't you move or a big tiger will come and eat you up."

They left the little girl and her baggage, and hurried away.

It was precisely noon, and no one was about. In rural Bali at this uncertain time in history, superstition still lay heavy on the land. A crossroads at noon was a place and an hour for witchcraft, it was generally thought, and to be found in such a place was considered dangerous, if only for one's reputation.

Ni Klinyar stood erect in the midst of her bundles of dowry, palpitating an obscene vocabulary of hues. Terror and fury raced over her in smears of magenta and viridian. The old man in white who seemed to appear from nowhere would have had no trouble recognizing her, even if he hadn't been Dayu Datu in disguise.

The old man was driving a bullock and cart, and peeling a

tangerine whose fragrance seemed to Klinyar to be the most beautiful thing on earth. He offered half of it to her, and immediately she calmed to a delicate pink, accepted it politely with her right hand, and after being bid only twice to begin eating, she put a wedge of the fruit into her mouth. It was an ordinary tangerine, and it was delicious. The old man smiled and Klinyar smiled back. Despite having no teeth at all, he was extraordinarily handsome, with kind, ironic eyes (with one brow arching high over a sleepy eyelid) and a frangipani flower tied into his delicate white wisp of a beard.

"Let's go, then," he said, and the next thing Klinyar knew, she was walking through the gate of a farmhouse in the southern hills, holding the hand of a tall woman. The same ironic eyes answered hers.

"Here we are. I bet you'd like a bath and some supper."

Over the next seven years, Dayu Datu treated Ni Klinyar like her own daughter, providing for all her needs with a steadiness of purpose that Klinyar could not disrupt. She taught Klinyar to perform her share of the household duties with skill and pride, and there was never any mention of school. Dayu Datu took care of all her instruction during those hours of the day and night when she had her "classes", and taught her the most interesting things: songs and chants that were nothing like what she would have learned in school; she taught her how to fly, how to eat glass, how to see great distances and become invisible, and how to change herself into, say, a household object, an animal, or a drawn symbol from a book; she taught her the holy books forward and backward. In all her studies Klinyar was diligent and joyful, and Dayu Datu responded with praise, thrilled at the rapid accomplishments of her protégée. Unwittingly, she grew fond of the child.

The house of Dayu Datu was an assortment of buildings surrounded by a great wall. The garden beyond the wall was ragged in appearance but bore all the usual fruits and flowers — bananas, chillies, coffee, morning glories, and many others. In discreet corners grew other plants, capable of producing itching, dysentery, hallucinations, death, and other such things as were required by her profession. The boundaries of her land were indeterminate: the forest marched deeply into her garden and was periodically burned back. In any case, there were no neighbors.

The interior of Dayu Datu's private quarters varied according to the witch's whims. At times the house was abysmally plain and poor, with furnishings of awkward design and unpleasant materials, placed as if by ill will in a small single room. A plywood cupboard covered in plaid plastic nearly blocked the only door. There was only one shelf, and it tipped at an angle to the floor, so that everything placed on it — broken combs, apple cores, etc. — tended to slide off. There was only one window and it wouldn't open, but conducted a glare at every hour of the day. Dripping pipes led to no source of water. The floor was of an unidentified material that creaked and yet was marshy, and it had holes and protuberances that were never in the same place. The walls met at unorthodox angles, and they oozed stains that suggested genitals and teeth.

This was the way Dayu Datu arranged her house when she was working on a professional problem or, which was more rare, if she had unexpected visitors.

At other times, during the evening classes, for instance, the interior became the library of a great country house, with high, well-squared walls and calm ceilings. It was a room lined with books that had the fantastic property of allowing one to enter the pictures and travel to amazing places. Thus Klinyar visited Paris, Disneyland, the shopping malls of Singapore and Dallas; thus, too, she knew the minimalist profundity of Antarctica and central Australia.

On library nights, Dayu Datu would dress in something long and dark, and sit in her armchair smoking, sipping from a small glass of hot arak. Klinyar usually sat on the floor, which was covered by a rich soft carpet. She was inclined to sprawl and review the contortionist exercises with which she began her day, and she did this in the spirit of a puppy who has just learned to please.

It was on library nights that Dayu Datu indulged in old age. A female witch's age cannot be determined and must never be fixed. As a woman she must always have at her command the arsenal of her sex: the confusing powers of virginity, the terrorism of menopause, the subterfuge of menstruation with its attendant toxins, the diplomatic resources of old age, and the magical aptitude of childhood. An adept like Dayu Datu would have in her charge vast permutations of gender, which, syncopated with the scale of age, afforded a great range of sexual expression. One of her most disturbing incarnations was that of Chalonarang — the protagonist of a mystery play that even now is still enacted all over Bali — in which she became a venerable male actor whose role was that of a rouged old woman and whose parure was fresh young leaves. Chalonarang's ritual function was to become the horrifying female beast Rangda, who is ultimately one of the dark faces of God — a big complicated role, and one she discharged with precision and chill, sometimes in as many as five different places at once and always with every biographical and local nuance intact.

As for Dayu Datu's own biography, her childhood is shrouded in rumor. She was born in Singaraja, in northern Bali, the child of a Brahman priest. Her mother was Chinese-Javanese, the daughter of a merchant and a princess — and although a bearer of royal blood herself, Dayu Datu's mother was but the third wife of the Brahman. His first wife had died childless. The second was exceedingly ambitious for the success of her own son, and it was well known that she hated the third wife.

What was not generally known, however, was that Dayu Datu had been born with a twin brother. The birth of male and female twins was an event of great import — highly auspicious if the birth was royal, but a gross impertinence if born to commoners: the entire village would become ritually impure for forty-two days, and the offending couple would be obliged to live in a little hut outside the village for the duration of this uncleanliness. Very often, one of the two twins did not survive more than a few minutes after its birth.

The birth of Dayu Datu and her brother caused havoc in the palace of the Brahman. The second wife was wild with jealousy and tried to have the third wife ostracized. A compromise was found by which the third wife was allowed to remain in the palace with her daughter, but the male twin was banished.

It was an uneasy truce. Dayu Datu's mother became slowly and quietly insane, dressing only in cobwebs, and addicted to opium. One day when Dayu Datu was about ten years old, the second wife — her mother's rival and torturer — was found murdered in her room. The instrument of murder was bizarre: a palm-leaf manuscript had been forced down her throat. It was half of a magical text; the other half was missing. And so was Dayu Datu.

The mystery was never solved. No sense could be had from Dayu Datu's mother, who also died soon afterward. The Brahman priest set off on a pilgrimage and was never heard from again. And nothing was heard of Dayu Datu for many years, until word began to circulate of a powerful witch who lived on the low southwestern mountain called Gunung Mumbul — that she was a Dayu (from Ida Ayu or "she is beautiful", the caste title of Brahman females) and that her magic was extraordinarily cruel and refined.

Dayu Datu's original physical make-up was slim and elegant, taller than average, with a sleepy eyelid caused by a blow to her brow in early adolescence, from a fall while learning to fly — a nerve was damaged, so that she could not open her left eyelid unless she arched her eyebrow. This gave her a look of haughty prescience that was quite involuntary, and it left a trace, because of this involuntary quality, in all her disguises. The effect of this facial asymmetry was disturbing to anyone who saw her: there could be fury or hilarity in her right eye, but in her left there was only reptilian detachment. Strangely enough, she never became aware of the impact of this peculiarity, nor realized that it was a signature. It seemed to her only an ungovernable defect in her facial equipment. When she was very tired, she sometimes tacked up her eyelid with the thorn of a rose.

Dayu Datu was a superb technician in the art of causing affliction, and her style was distinctive. She excelled at transformations and in an instant could turn herself into, say, an air conditioner, or a can of foot powder, or a school of sharks. She amused herself with magic at a distance: making animals fart helplessly, for instance, or causing birds to molt out of season. She could jam staplers and sever nerves and cause corks to rot in bottles, gums to bleed, and planes to fall from the sky. Her weapons were the small and large things across time that can cause a person to lose faith in life.

In some ways, Dayu Datu was conventional. She kept dogs, owls, hawks, and crows, and she had a houseful of disciples, all female like herself. She acquired them as a matter of course, for the perpetuation of her art. She took no personal interest in her clients nor in the assignments they brought her, except as a set of clinical circumstances against which to exercise her craft. She was expensive, not for love of money, since she had no love for anything and had no need for money, but because it was a convention among black magicians to be expensive — and she was very expensive, as was commensurate with her status. She used the money to ornament her students, for she found that it kept them on edge to have an appetite for luxury. And sometimes, if she felt that she'd accumulated an annoyingly large sum of money, she would go in disguise to an illicit cockfight, to lure a man into losing everything he had, and then gambling it all away just for the pleasure of losing money herself.

The advent of Klinyar into her life created something new and disturbing for Dayu Datu, for as we have already mentioned, she had become fond of her. Dayu Datu was confused by the sensations Klinyar aroused in her, and sometimes she wondered if perhaps she was ill. If Klinyar was too long away from her company, she was distressed, and if Klinyar came running up to her to show her something, she felt giddy, although she never allowed these feelings to show. Sometimes Dayu Datu thought she ought to kill Klinyar and rid herself of this disruptive presence, but no sooner did she begin to contemplate the murder than she'd become very ill indeed: fitful breathing and moaning, accompanied by excessive watering of the eyes and facial spasms. Eventually she discovered that she felt best when she concentrated on Klinyar's well-being. And so Ni Klinyar became the witch's most precious pupil.

MUDITA GREW UP in Mameling in the care of Rajin and Madé Kerti, believing them to be his parents, and he did not lack anything his real parents would have given him. From Madé Kerti he learned to grow rice and build walls and play a variety of musical instruments. From Rajin he learned to be courteous and helpful, and brave in the face of suffering. It was from Ni Sabuk, his grandmother, that he learned about the large things of the world.

"We are Balinese, Mudita," she told him, "that is, human beings. Our work is to take care of life in the world."

"How big is the world, Nini?"

"Oh, very big — much bigger than Mameling. There are the mountains far to the north and the sea far to the south. The mountains are the beginning of all things, and the sea is the end of all things."

"And we're in the middle?"

"Yes, we are. Right in the middle of it all. Here we have everything we need."

Mudita was a happy child. He was well loved in the village and had many friends, not only among boys of his own age, but among small children and the elderly as well. He was also an exceptionally handsome boy. He had inherited his mother's silky skin and enchanting smile; but what distinguished his own special beauty was the legibility of his face and the sweetness of character that animated it. He had, within the balance of his features, a peculiarity much prized by the Balinese — a small mole at the outer edge of his right eyebrow, which added an elegant adornment to whatever expression lit his face.

It must be added, too, that his body smelled of cinnamon, and his breath of freshly husked rice. But, best of all, he had no idea that there was anything special about himself at all.

As Mudita was growing up, so too was Mameling.

One day, Mudita asked his grandmother, "Nini, is Bali the whole world?"

Ni Sabuk clacked her loom. "In a way. Why do you ask?"

"I saw some strange-looking people coming out of the palace today. They were very pale and I thought they must be sick people asking for help, but somebody said they were tourists — they come from beyond Bali. Is that true, Nini?"

"That could be true."

"But how? You said Bali was the whole world. Are tourists from outside the world?"

"It's like this, 'Dita," she said, drawing with her finger on the palm of her hand. "The world is like a circle. Here in the center is Bali. Then around Bali is Java. People from Java look like normal human beings. Then all around outside is Holland. The people from there are called Dutch and they are very big and pale, it's true."

"Are they human beings?"

"So they say."

"What were Dutch people doing at the palace?"

"They're all aristocrats," said Ni Sabuk. "They like to travel around staying in palaces."

One day the young prince of Mameling summoned a dozen of the most influential villagers. After they'd all sipped glasses of coffee and lit up the free cigarettes, he told them, "The future of Mameling is in tourism. Our foreign guests are powerful people in their own countries. They do us a great honor by showing so much interest in our culture. Do you know what culture is?"

There was a short silence.

"Culture is the way we do things. The tourists do things differently. They have a different culture — a very poor one, which is why they are so interested in ours. They have lots of money, yes, but they know nothing about the gods, they can't dance or play music, except for their own sort on radios, they don't understand rice, and many of them don't even eat rice."

This produced a roar of laughter from the men.

"So we have to make the tourists feel welcome and comfortable, and provide them with the things they need. Now, what do tourists need? And what can we provide them with?"

A rhetorical pause while the puzzled group sat waiting.

"They need to buy things. And after they buy things, they need a cold drink of beer. They need to eat and sleep, like we do, but they need to eat in a tourist way and sleep in a tourist way. And they don't know how to go to the river."

Another roar of laughter.

"They need bathrooms, like the Chinese in Denpasar. We'll talk about all this eating and sleeping and bathing in a minute. Now, what do the tourists want to buy? They will try to buy anything, everything. But we're poor people!"

This was another rhetorical device. The prince was in fact very rich, and it was the villagers who were poor. No one dared mention this, of course.

"We must use our heads and our hands to make things for the tourists to buy," the prince went on. "Some of us can paint. Let's make paintings for the tourists. Some of us can carve. Let's make sculpture for the tourists — or jewelry, if we're good at that. Perhaps our children can dance. Let's have them dance for the tourists! But let us protect our heirlooms. Don't sell your krisses. Don't sell your silver offering bowls and the fine old carvings from your house temples. Let us protect our heritage, our *culture!*"

They let this pass, too. It was well known that the prince had made spectacular sales of palace treasures.

"Now. How do we make the tourists comfortable? We all have a bit of extra space in our compounds to build a guest house. How do we do this? First we get a permit, and then we build a nice little house and put in a new bed — it must new, with a new mattress, pillow, and blanket — and on the porch we give them a chair to sit on. That's right, a chair, just like the one I'm sitting one, but it doesn't have to be as nice as this one. This is from the court of Yogyakarta and is three hundred years old." Actually it was Dutch, from Denpasar, from around 1932. "You can put a little bamboo chair on the porch for your tourist, and a little bamboo table for his glass of tea."

One of the men asked the prince if he could explain about the bathroom.

"Very important. It has to be inside the little guest house. That's right, they want the bathroom indoors. And nobody in your family may use it when you have your tourist living there. And you must give your tourist his own private towel. Now here's how it works …"

And so Mameling entered the age of "cultural tourism". Soon foreigners were seen everywhere, standing in people's way at the market, milling around in temples, walking half undressed and sweaty through the countryside, and forever holding black boxes in front of their faces. The foreigners were ugly, but they were very friendly, and hilariously stupid, particularly with their money, of which they seemed to have unlimited amounts. All of this meant great changes for Mameling.

The village became a small town. It joined the great Republic of Indonesia, and representatives came from the government to pave the roads, install electricity, and build clinics and schools. A television was set up on a pole in front of the post office. Somebody bought a refrigerator and an ice-making box, and then somebody else did, and then one villager bought his own private television, and the very next day the prince also bought his own private television, and the race was on.

Meanwhile the tourists were pouring in, and people in Mameling were making a lot of money. Those who could paint, did; and those who couldn't bought cheap and sold high, and still the tourists were delighted with their bargains. Little girls became little *legong* dancers and grew into big *legong* dancers, and more than one eloped with an enchanted tourist, bringing riches and heartache to her family. "Homestays" suddenly appeared in every back yard, and soon materialized in the rice fields like big, luxurious rice granaries. Some of the old people objected to having toilets in rice granaries, but the younger people explained that they weren't actually rice granaries — they just looked like them, because that's what the tourists wanted.

"Who'd want to sleep in a stuffy place like that with all those bugs?" marveled the old people.

"Oh, but it's very nice up there, come look," said the young people.

"Ha! I wouldn't go up there and stand above the temple shrines. Take your own chances."

One old quarter of town that had always been known as Abian Cheleng (Pig Fields) prospered so quickly that its residents decided to change its name to Tumbensugih, which is Balinese for nouveau riche. The richest man in Tumbensugih was Gdé Kedampal, who as a young boy had been a porter. By working hard and saving carefully, he was able to buy materials to make a pushcart. Soon he had a minivan and married a local girl. When his son, Wayan Buyar, was learning to walk, Gdé Kedampal already had three vans with three paid drivers. By the time Wayan Buyar lost his virginity (to a goose), Gdé Kedampal had a prosperous transport business, with a fleet of air-conditioned buses. Later, he branched out into packing-and-shipping and logistics.

Many *warung* — little stands, sometimes no more than a little table, where one can buy rice, coffee, cigarettes, arak, candy, and other lovely unhealthy things — became *rumah makan*, Indonesian diners, and they all served cold beer, fried chicken, and "Indonesian Favorites" and "Western Favorites" with imaginative spellings. The Balinese found this food revolting, but they served it cheerfully and made friends with the tourists. Mudita shyly practiced his English with the tourists he met at the traditional *warung*.

For *warung* persisted, as did much of the old way of life. People still communed with the gods and held huge, complicated rituals; they still plowed their fields with cows and cooked their rice over smoky wood fires. Rajin and Madé Kerti watched the world changing beyond their house gates, but life within the compound was much the same, except that their oil lamps were replaced by naked light bulbs, so that Mudita could study more easily in the evenings.

"Ah, technology is a wonderful thing," said Madé Kerti every time he switched on the lights. "You know, 'Jin," he said to his wife one evening, "we're very lucky that the tourists have come to Mameling."

"Is that so," snapped Rajin. "How, exactly?"

"Look at all the progress they've brought. Lights! Roads! Schools! Don't think it's like this everywhere in Bali."

"The tourists built the roads? I didn't see that."

"No, of course not, they didn't build the roads themselves. Our government did, so the tourists could get here more easily."

"And raise the price of everything beyond reach, and teach our young people to drink beer and wear trousers."

"Does Mudita drink beer?" said Madé Kerti, suddenly concerned.

"Ask him."

"Mudita! Mudita, my dear, come here for just a minute."

Mudita stood up in the patch of light where he'd been studying and walked over to the pavilion where Rajin and Madé Kerti were sitting comfortably in the gloom. Mudita sat between his parents.

"Yes, Bapa?" He gave Madé Kerti a beautiful smile.

"Mudita, have you ever had beer?"

"Oh, yes! But it has to be very cold or it's not so nice."

"Mudita, I'm sorry to ask you this, but where do you get the money to buy beer? Do you know that a bottle of beer costs more than your mother makes at the market in a whole day?"

"Oh, but I don't buy it myself. I'm invited by my friends."

"What friends are these?"

Rajin cut in. "Tourists! Mudita, last night when you came home, your breath stank. I don't want you to smell like a tourist."

Madé Kerti put his arm around Mudita's neck. "I'm glad you have generous friends, 'Dita. But just this, to please your mother: after you've been with the tourists, brush your teeth, okay? Now don't look so sad."

Mudita took Rajin's hand and pressed it to his face.

"Mudita," she said, "don't cry, I'm not angry with you. Come here."

Rajin and Madé Kerti began to feel that perhaps Siladri had been right in foreseeing great changes in the world. Life became hard for them. Their quiet lane was paved, and motorbikes and vans roared past their house; a bar opened across the street, and deep into the night they heard the thumping of dreadful music. Ni Sabuk ignored these changes, saying only, "At least we have enough to eat and nobody's disappearing in the night." But one day Rajin and Madé Kerti fell very ill.

Mudita was frightened by their sudden infirmity. Each day they seemed to age a year, and they quickly became old and frail. It became clear that they would soon die.

They lay side by side in the east pavilion, where the elderly sleep and young people receive their rites of passage and where the dead lie before they are buried or cremated.

"Rajin, my love, do you think we'll ever get out of here?"

"One way or another," she said. "We can't stay here forever."

"'Jin."

"Yah?"

"I think I'd better tell Mudita about Siladri."

"Yah."

When Mudita had finished bathing and feeding them both, had smoothed a clean cloth over each of them, and sat down to tell them of his day, Madé Kerti told him to fetch the strongbox from the cupboard.

Inside were their few bits of treasure: Rajin's jewelry, cloth woven by Ni Sabuk, shells and bits of string and several loops of Chinese coins, and a little leather box. It was this box that Madé Kerti told Mudita to take out and open. Inside was a heavy gold ring.

"This ring was made for you by your father," said Madé Kerti.

Mudita stared at him.

"No, my dear, not me. I am your father's brother. I wanted to wait until you were older before telling you, but there's not much time, and I'm so tired."

Madé Kerti paused and began dozing. Mudita watched every small breath until he woke again.

"Ah, Mudita, you're wearing your ring. I thought for a minute it was Siladri."

"Siladri?"

"Siladri is your father. Now listen. He lives on Gunung Kawi. Mémé and I will die soon. Let us spend a year together in the earth before you cremate us. As soon as we are buried, Mudita, go to Gunung Kawi and tell Siladri we have died, so that he may know he is ritually unclean. He must be told, Mudita, because he went there to become a *dukuh*, a holy man."

Tears of confusion and grief swam in Mudita's eyes, and he clamped his mouth tight to keep his lips from trembling. He kept his face down and rubbed the ring on his finger.

"Mémé is your mother's sister. Your mother is a wonderful girl."

Kadek, said Rajin to herself.

"And you have a cousin," said Madé Kerti.

"Kusuma Sari," Rajin whispered. Her eyes filled with tears. "A beautiful baby girl."

"If only we could see her!" said Madé Kerti.

Mudita sat up and said. "You will. I'll go to Gunung Kawi and bring them all here. I promise you."

"Oh, Mudita, hurry."

"I'll leave tomorrow."

That night Madé Kerti and Rajin had this conversation:

    Rajin: "'Dé, do you think we'll see them?"

    Kerti: "Yah."

    Rajin: "'Dé."

    Kerti: "Yah."

    Rajin: "I don't think I'll see them."

    Kerti: "Yah."

    Rajin: "'Dé. Say something else."

    Kerti: "Yah, okay. I'm here with you."

    Rajin: "Say my name, 'Dé."

    Kerti: "I'm here with you … my Rajin."

    Mudita heard them whispering and came with a lamp.

    "Bring her to me, Mudita," said Madé Kerti.

    "I will. I'll be leaving in a few hours."

    "No, 'Dita. Bring me Rajin."

    Mudita lifted the wisp of Rajin and laid her next to the wisp of Madé Kerti.

    "Thank you, 'Dita. You're a good boy," said Madé Kerti. "Good night, my dear."

    "I'll come see you before I leave."

    "Yah."

Mudita got up as soon as the night began to fade. He packed a small shoulder bag and closed the door behind him. Walking quietly through the gloom, he approached the east pavilion. He found his parents lying dead in each other's arms, foreheads touching, feet wrapped in feet, Rajin's hand wrapped in Madé Kerti's hand and pressed against his chest.

As MADÉ KERTI had instructed, husband and wife were buried together, wrapped in a single shroud. Ni Sabuk directed the rituals. When the last bit of earth was patted over their grave and the other villagers were quietly departing, Mudita sat down on the grave and cried like a child.

Ni Sabuk sat beside him on the grave of her son. She herself did not weep. "Now they'll have some peace and quiet."

Mudita sobbed into his grandmother's hands.

"This is your first sadness, 'Dita. It's always the worst. But it promises happiness later. We can't skip any of it."

Mudita left for Gunung Kawi the day after the burial. It was the month of Sasih Kapat, when the trees are in flower, and the grasses, too: a white cloud of blossoms waved over the long *alang-alang* grass that grows on the slopes of the river gorges. All the world seemed to be in blossom, and the air was alive with the big, papery flowers of the waru tree. Mudita, now seventeen and still a virgin, was unaware of the lore that says one may not make love until the waru flowers fall in the late afternoon, the hour when the light deepens and the colors blaze forth from walls, leaves, flowers, bowls, and doorsills, and a glow rises from the earth.

Mudita left at dawn, as is proper to all important beginnings, but it took him much of the morning to get out of Mameling. As he passed a *warung*, some friends called him over to join them.

"'Dita," one of them said, "lend me some money until next week, can you?"

"Of course. How much do you need?"

"Can you give me a ringgit?"

"Of course." It was all Mudita had.

"You're a wonderful person," said Mudita's friend, tucking the money into his belt.

"Have some coffee, where are you going?" said another.

"No, thanks, I have to meet someone," said Mudita. "I'll see you all soon."

And so Mudita set off for Gunung Kawi without coffee and carrying nothing but his gold ring.

He took the road north out of town, already busy with traffic. Buses filled with tourists from the tourist hives on the south coast roared past — big American-sized buses like windowed refrigerators full of plump, powdery fruit. There were little *bemo* trucks full to the edges and dragging their bottoms, crammed with market women and market wares — bulging baskets of vegetables, sacks of rice, and hens and ducks tied together by their feet — and hanging off the back would be four or five young men shouting and laughing. There were empty *bemos* going back toward Mameling, clanging in their lightness as they skimmed the asphalt waves of the road.

Mudita thought he would catch a *bemo* as far as the mountain town of Pujung and then inquire about another *bemo* to the village nearest the forests of Gunung Kawi. He had only a vague idea of where these forests were — somewhere to the northeast — but he hoped that with luck he would be able to locate his father's mountain retreat by late afternoon, at about the time the flowers would be falling from the waru tree.

And then he remembered that he had no money.

But the morning was fresh, and it was pleasant to walk, and time was big and light with Mudita. He hadn't been on this road since his class hiked to the holy spring at Sebatu on their last day of junior school. Was the road paved then? He couldn't remember. Certainly it had not been well traveled — his new rubber sandals had been useless by the time the class returned. He recalled the look on his mother's — that is, his aunt's — face when he had showed her his ripped thongs: a curtain of quiet drawn over a flash of fatigue. This time, he told himself, he would walk through the rice fields.

Mudita nearly fell as he slipped into a narrow irrigation gully. He was thinking of Rajin and Madé Kerti — and his real parents; would he remember them when he saw them? Mudita felt faint.

Just now, he thought, I don't really exist. Nobody knows exactly where I am. I'm like the air. He realized that he was thirsty and he headed toward a bamboo grove, a sure sign that there would be a river nearby.

Rivers descend, but they lead to the mountains as much as they lead to the sea, thought Mudita. It would be pleasant to find a spring and then walk out the hot part of the day in an upstream trek.

Now the rice fields are steaming, shimmering white around him. There is no one about. It must be lunchtime, Mudita thinks. There's not a farmer in sight. The buzz in his head stretches around him in a wide, circular haze. His legs feel as if they are made of mud. A skinny dog trips past, tongue and sphincter wagging; Mudita follows him into the crisp shade of the bamboo grove. Nearby, he hopes, there will be a hamlet, and that means hospitality — a glass of hot tea or even coffee, a chance to sit for a moment and talk with his host about the slow and remarkable things in the life of the house: the bloom of a particular plant or grandchild; vagaries of the season; the way things used to be. Mudita imagines himself seated on a porch and his temperature slowly returning to normal as he makes note of the faces who are providing him with this rest. He would look around and notice with what care the courtyard has been swept, and maybe that a hen limps. Soon he would be asked to stay and eat rice, and he'd stand and exchange cordial wishes of farewell.

Mudita bends his heart to such a house.

In the near distance he hears the wooden clack of a cowbell beyond the rich stands of banana trees, yams, and razory elephant grass. From far away he hears the cool speech of a river below. Mudita's bowels are suddenly peppery with fatigue, and he decides to go first to the river, and then search for hospitality once he's refreshed.

Easily he finds a path leading down to the river, slippery over roots and rocks; he follows it eagerly down through a tiny cloud of colored moths, past a shy brown snake, around a congress of ferns. The sound of the water is strong now — it seems to come from beneath his feet — and his arms and legs stiffen with the rising chill. The sunlight barely seeps through the deepening gloom of green. The world has grown mossy, the stones black and slippery as the path drops straight down.

At last he reaches the narrow, pebbly bank of the stream. As he expected, the place is deserted, for it is nearly noon; but to judge by the storm of footprints, it must have been shrill with people bathing and washing their clothes not more than half an hour before. By his foot he sees a rotted half coconut shell with a smear of laundry soap in it; on the other side of the river is a single rubber sandal. In this echo-populated solitude, Mudita turns discreetly to the wall of the gorge and takes off his clothes, then he wobbles carefully into the water and, turning southward, downstream toward the sea, he hides his beautiful bottom in the river.

Mudita did not find hospitality that day or that night, nor did he see a single human being. For seven days and seven nights, Mudita walked toward Gunung Kawi, and not once did he eat or drink or sleep. He wandered the ravines and forests, his heart focused on finding the father and mother he did not remember.

He climbed through deep crystalline nights, his eyes full of the starry sky and his body warm with exertion. Once he felt as if he was climbing toward the sky itself. There were long purple afternoons filled with rain and the sound of a maternal purring. Sometimes he saw the war horses of the God Indra, and he followed them through the milky rain. Sometimes the afternoons were soft with sunlight, and he was showered with the flowers of waru trees, and when this happened, he was filled with a longing for honey.

In the depths of the seventh night, Mudita knew he was lost, and he was slashed with fear. There was no moon and it was so dark that he could hardly find his face with his hands. His heart rattled in his chest and he began to weep out loud, calling for his mother and then for his father, but he was nearly crazed with starvation and fatigue, and his words made no sound.

The world around him was black and noisy with movement, and Mudita thought he was drowning. I have fallen into the sea, he told himself. He felt his mind float past him, and he gave it up to death, pronouncing with his heart:

Ocean, I am you.

His arms floated upward and his legs swam in the dark, stupidly. All bliss melted from him and blended with the night. And then, at the end of his fingertips there were — other fingertips: tiny hands as black as the night itself. Oh, the night has hands, he thought. He let his wrists rise into the clasp of a forest monkey.

Mudita rose to follow, his hands now wrapped in the soft grasp of the monkey. His heart bounced slowly behind him like a dumb thing, growing heavier and heavier, and soon he felt his feet float away behind him, lingering and dangling behind his heart. Mudita drifted on an oceanic night, a flickering night, a night striated, a night striped with a coat of darkness and light, as if he were riding on the back of a tiger. In his dreaming he became the saddle cloth of a galloping tiger, under the heels of a forest monkey, and still he could not faint or die.

On the morning of the eighth day he found himself high in the spacious forests of the mountains. He walked among the tall trees as if through an aquarium of sunlight. The air was bright and humming with fragrance, and he heard singing. Oh, I must be in heaven, he thought. Butterflies and orchids fluttered before his eyes, and the singing came closer, traveling on a breeze with the breath of grasses. And then he saw the girl, a wonderful mountain girl with a basket of flowers under her arm. Mudita felt himself hovering in the sunlight.

"Who are you?" said Kusuma Sari. "And what brings you to Gunung Kawi?"

"My name is Mudita," he said, "and I'm gathering honey." And then he sank to the ground.

A few moments later, Mudita tasted honey in his mouth and heard the voice of Kusuma Sari, lilting in the brightness overhead. " ... but the easiest thing to do is simply speak directly to the queen bee. She makes all the important decisions, and if you ask nicely, and don't ask for too much, she'll get her helpers to break off a bit of the honeycomb for you and you don't even have to climb the tree. I can see that you haven't had much luck finding honey lately. Why don't you let me show you how?"

Mudita opened his eyes and licked the honey from his lips and looked at the face of the girl — so lively and warm, so round and kind. He said, "Forgive me. I am looking for Dukuh Siladri."

"Then I will take you to him. These are his woods, and these flowers are for his prayers, and very nearby is his house."

"Please. In just a minute. It's so good to rest here," said Mudita. "Is this Gunung Kawi?"

"Yes, you poor thing. Oh, I think you're very tired." Kusuma Sari brushed the hair from Mudita's face. "Where have you come from?"

Mudita closed his eyes and sighed as the sun washed across his face. He felt more honey being tucked into his mouth, and he heard the wind in the trees high above him. He felt Kusuma Sari's face close to his, and heard her whisper, "Never mind, just lie there until you feel better." He felt cool leaves being pressed on his forehead. He heard Kusuma Sari humming as she bathed his wrists with leaves, and he opened his eyes a little and saw her laying more leaves over his feet. He saw her hair come undone and slide down her back, and he saw the curve of her neck, her fine shoulders, and the satiny skin of her arms as she rubbed the leaves between his toes. He saw the motion of her breasts, and he watched her lips moving in a little song as she spread the leaves over his calves, and suddenly Mudita was feeling very strong. He closed his eyes again and let his heart lift into the trees.

As for Kusuma Sari, she thought she had never touched a more precious creature in her life. He's like a calf, she thought, but also like a rose, and a young lion. She grew warm and happy. She stroked his feet and his arms, and placed some rose petals behind his ears — and then, without thinking, she kissed his cheeks.

Mudita opened his eyes and took Kusuma Sari's hand. Overhead, the wind moved through the trees and grasses, filling the air with tiny flowers. They stayed that way for a long while, until she said, "Shall we go, then?"

Kusuma Sari led Mudita slowly through the forest. She carried her basket of flowers under one arm and slid the other around his waist. He leaned lightly against her and let his arm drift up around her shoulders. The forest shimmered around them.

"It's not far," said Kusuma Sari, smiling up at him.

"What's not far?" Mudita would have been happy to walk with her in the forest forever.

"The house — have you forgotten?"

"Oh, yes. No! I haven't forgotten. That is, I'm sorry. I thought I was dreaming."

Just then, they came to the walls of a large courtyard, and Kusuma Sari took Mudita's hand. Mudita thought he'd never seen such an inviting house.

There was a great banyan tree in front of the gate, and from inside the courtyard, flowering vines spilled over the walls. As they walked through the gate, a kingfisher swooped and perched on the head of Kusuma Sari, flapping turquoise above her hair. A fat white puppy, a pair of kid goats, a heron, all came to greet her. Butterflies bathed her path. A monkey sat in a frangipani tree, staring at Kusuma Sari as if he were her fiancé, and when she put out her arms to him, he leapt into her embrace and passed his hand over her cheek. Mudita saw a huge tiger lolling in the shade by the kitchen.

"So many animals," said Mudita, still light-headed.

Kusuma Sari laughed. "Do you think so?" She brought Mudita to a fine old pavilion where a man was reading at a small table. "Father, we have a guest."

Mudita gazed at the man and saw that he was slender, with graying hair tucked up under a white headcloth. He noted that the man wore spectacles and had slim hands, and for a moment he thought he was looking at Ni Sabuk. Mudita greeted him respectfully, with his hands pressed together and raised before his face.

"Mudita," whispered Dukuh Siladri. "Mudita, my precious child. Come here. Come to me. Ah, you're like a bird, Mudita, just like your mother. That's right, put your head right here, my darling. Sari! Your brother has come home to us. Come pet him. You see? This is his ring, the one I made for him when he was a baby. Oh, my Mudita."

Over the next few hours there was much talking and rejoicing and weeping as Siladri and his son exchanged news of Kadek and Rajin and Madé Kerti. Kusuma Sari held and comforted them in turn, and she cried with them. She wept with her face high and her mouth open, like Madé Kerti.

At last they became calm and Siladri took the hands of his children and said, "So, then. Here we are, our little family. And I see that you love each other. Am I right? That makes me very happy. You are cousins; it is very good. Now, Sari, take Mudita to the kitchen and give him something to eat, and eat together with him, like husband and wife. Don't wait for me, I have not prayed yet. Did you remember to bring my flowers?"

In the kitchen, Kusuma Sari poked the fire and moved some pots and soon was ladling out rice porridge for Mudita. They passed the bowl back and forth between them and fed each other with a palm-leaf spoon. Thus, in the old ways of Bali, they were married.

Mudita leaned against the sacks of rice and felt his back and the back of his head melt against their shape. He felt his gaze slide down to his knees and roll, revolving toward Kusuma Sari like a honeycomb prisoner. He felt his cheeks slide down his face and nestle into his shoulders, and he felt his jaws grind comfortably into position and soon from the deep composure of his face there came a gentle snore. Mudita was asleep for the first time in seven days. From time to time, his fingertips lifted in soft interrogation into the air. Kusuma Sari moved the betelnut box next to him for protection and went outside, closing the kitchen door carefully behind her, to catch the waru blossoms beginning to fall in the courtyard.

Time turned around the lovers and held them in a spell of flavors. The winter rain came, soaking the mountain in an underwater light of blues and greens; the sky, when they could see it, was lavender. In the early mornings, Mudita and Kusuma Sari went to the river to bathe, inching down the path now treacherous and greasy with mud. As the climbed down, they grabbed on to wet black roots, and sometimes their faces were nudged by orchids.

All winter it rained from mid-morning to late afternoon, and everything was soft and wet. Stone walls grew mosses of emerald velvet. Clothes became speckled with mold. Kusuma Sari kept the kitchen fire going all day and heaped up the embers at night.

At the equinox, the air grew calm and clear. Mudita dug up the gardens, and Kusuma Sari planted summer vegetables and scattered the beds with marigold seeds. Piglets were born, the deer multiplied, and the coffee trees were snowy with blossoms. Then came the cool, dry months of summer. The gardens grew tall; vines sagged with tomatoes, pumpkins, and snake beans; bougainvillea and roses blazed from the eaves of the house. The days were chilly, dusty, and brilliant, and the nights were cold and bright.

One night, Mudita and Kusuma Sari lay wrapped in a cocoon of rough blankets, pressing their feet together.

"Mudita, is there a difference for you between making love at night and making love in the morning?"

Mudita thought a moment and smiled. "Yes, there is."

"Well? What is it?"

"In the morning, it's like a single color," he said. "And at night it's multicolor."

Kusuma Sari turned and looked out through the gaps in the timbers of their house at the night sky. "Why is it that everything I see looks like you?"

"What do you see out there that looks like me?" said Mudita.

"The stars."

"The stars look like me?"

"And earlier this evening I saw my face in the water jug and that looked like you, too. How can that be?"

Mudita stared at Kusuma Sari. A cold light showed the outline of her ear. "I don't know," he said. "Nothing I know looks like you. To me you look so much like yourself that if I can't see you, I don't want to look at anything else."

Kusuma Sari closed herself around Mudita and breathed in the cinnamon warmth of his skin. Mudita took a lock of her long hair, wrapped it around his wrist, and murmured, "And now what are you thinking?"

"I was thinking that — oh, it's very hard to explain. It's that whatever is happening right now is always moving on with us." She slid her foot along Mudita's leg. "Do you understand what I mean?"

"Not yet. Tell me," said Mudita.

"Whatever is, right now, changes every instant, but the present itself, or whatever contains the present, is always with us, no matter what. The present is like goodness: it never runs out."

"Do you think the present will always contain us?" said Mudita.

"Oh yes."

"And our mothers? Does the present contain our mothers still?"

"You mean the dead?" she said softly.

"Well, yes."

"But of course it does. Where else would they be?"

"Then that means," said Mudita, raising himself on an elbow, "that the present is, well, enormous. Big enough to get lost in."

Kusuma Sari burst out laughing and then covered her mouth. "You sounded like our father when you said that. And I know just what he'd say."

"What?"

"He'd say — well, actually I've heard him say this — he'd say that some people get lost inside their own hearts. Think of it!"

"I would like to be lost inside your heart," said Mudita, lying down again.

"Inside my heart you would never be lost."

W AYAN BUYAR sucks a piece of meat from his teeth. He is lolling with his friends in the shade of a pavilion, his body, soft and sweaty, staining the silk of the cushions; a fat gold chain hangs from his neck. The midday heat buzzes white. One of his friends is telling an elaborate lie about his relations with the wife of a prominent merchant; another is tweezing his whiskers with two sliding coins. Two others are lying down with their legs flopped over each other, one of them adding commentary in an undertone, the other already asleep and snoring.

Wayan Buyar is hardly listening to his friend. He knows the story; he told it himself not even a month ago. It was a lie then, too, but very satisfying to tell — succulent and glistening. They'd all feasted on it. Wayan Buyar slid his forefinger along the gold chain around his neck and released a fart. He rolled over, turning his back on the story, and said, "I sent her away last night, the sorry old slit. She can't stay away from me. I told her: Virgins only, come back when you're a virgin."

The storyteller threw a cushion at him. "You pig, Buyar. I hear you have to pay your dog to hold still for you."

"What a disgusting imagination you have," said Wayan Buyar without moving. "You make me feel faint."

"How long has it been since you fucked a human being, Buyar?" said someone else.

"What do you people know about sex?" said Wayan Buyar. "I have been, you know, a married man, many times over."

This elicited a round of hooting.

"How many times, b'li?"

"Eight." Wayan Buyar said this in a thick voice. In truth, he had been married seven times, but he wasn't sure whether this was something to brag about; each of his wives had fled within a couple of weeks.

"Oh my goodness, eight times laid!"

Wayan Buyar was not an attractive man. He was beetle-browed, and there were wide spaces between his teeth. His body was flabby and cheesy-smelling. His first marriage had been the outcome of arrangements between his father, Gdé Kedampal, and another rich merchant — a financial merger rather than a love match. The girl was tall and timid and sour-spirited. On their wedding night, as Wayan Buyar tore away at her virginity, she had become violently sick; for this impudence he beat her brutally about the head. There was no love between them, and very soon Wayan Buyar cast about for a second wife. (The local prince had five, an expression of royal flair to which Wayan Buyar, a commoner, feverishly aspired.)

When he brought home his second wife, a pretty and playful local girl who sold betelnut in the town square, he lavished upon her the jewels and costly clothes of his first wife and ordered his first wife to move to the kitchen. She did so, but the next day moved again, back to her father's house, taking the rest of her dowry with her.

Wayan Buyar was at once furious and relieved by this desertion. He apologized to his father, but Buyar was too busy enjoying his new wife to appreciate his father's disappointment. Wayan Buyar spoiled the girl with rich food and toys, but when she refused to let him urinate on her, he locked her in a closet for the weekend. She left on the Monday, taking with her as much silver as she could hide in her clothes.

His third wife was already four months pregnant when her parents pleaded with Gdé Kedampal to force his son to marry the girl. Wayan Buyar refused: although she was a sweet-tempered and compliant girl, she had a harelip; Buyar's interest in her had been not so much personal as practical. But his father was mortified by the entreaties of her parents, and he imposed an ultimatum: Wayan Buyar must marry the girl or be disinherited; he could always look for a prettier wife later. Buyar finally agreed, but exacted revenge: on the night of their wedding he kicked the girl's belly until she miscarried. The girl went home the next day on a litter, and that evening she died. Gdé Kedampal, overriding the objections of his son, sent the family a bullock in recompense for their grief.

Wayan Buyar found that he was getting a reputation. He took to traveling to the towns on the coast, where he was a stranger. His conspicuous wealth quickly won him a fourth wife, a nice girl from a simple farming family. He strummed her with popular songs and bought her a pair of earrings, and later he bought a television set for her parents.

"But they have no electricity," said the girl, who was called Manis.

"I don't care, I love you," said Wayan Buyar.

The wedding procedures went forward as if Wayan Buyar, too, were a virgin. His father paid a formal call on the family of Manis — an extravagant expedition with a retinue of twenty servants and followers and several motorcars. (The great number of guests strained the hospitality of Manis's family and forced them to mortgage their rice crop for the next two years.) Gdé Kedampal carried out the ritual request for the daughter and became very jolly with Manis's father, courtly with Manis's mother, and almost flirtatious with Manis's grandmother. He doted on Manis herself, and the entire occasion was all that a wedding should be except that Wayan Buyar himself was not present. There was an important cockfight in another part of Bali that weekend, and he sent, with his regrets, his kris to take his place.

The marriage rituals thus technically completed, the bride set off that night for her husband's house, accompanied by her father-in-law and an escort of twenty tipsy retainers, seven of whom offered, on the long ride home, to perform the office of their young master to his bride. When at last they reached Tumbensugih and the young bride was shown her new home, there was still no sign of the bridegroom. Manis retired with her husband's kris lying beside her, and she cried herself to sleep. When Wayan Buyar finally arrived home a week later, he was accompanied by wife number five.

Within three weeks, Wayan Buyar found himself again without a wife to cheer his nights.

His sixth and seventh wives were a set of twins from Minnesota who could not bear to be apart. This triangular marriage lasted six days, and all records of it have been destroyed, although there are stories still told in the *warung* around Mameling that Wayan Buyar had been molested by the pair and forced to sign over to them a substantial piece of real estate on the coast — part of his fourth wife's dowry, perhaps.

The heat of the day was beginning to fade. In the pavilion, Wayan Buyar sat up, suddenly very awake, very sad. He spoke to his friends, gazing into the air. "I'm a loving man, a man who should be married. Somewhere there's a woman worthy of my love. An old-fashioned girl, kind and beautiful, who can appreciate —"

"I've seen her," said the one who'd been tweezing his whiskers.

"What?"

" 'An old-fashioned girl, kind and beautiful'. I've seen her at the market in Kayuambua. She exists."

"Oh, you make me feel so tired," said Buyar, who hated not to be the first to know anything.

"I'm not kidding you. I've seen her four times there. She's a mountain girl — sells honey, marigolds, roses."

"She sounds very much like my sort of woman. Pure, competent, unspoiled by old wives' tales about women's rights and all that."

"B'li Wayan, that girl is out of the question."

"— who would be a companion to a man as he came into his full powers, a champion and defender of a man's true worth —"

"— true millions —"

"You are all beginning to sound like hangers-on," said Wayan Buyar to the horizon.

His friends registered this change of tone, and, careful of their favor, they assumed a more courtly demeanor. All were awake now, sitting up. One who had been lolling next to Wayan Buyar quietly slid down to the mat. The chin-tweezer, a lanky and dour-looking young man called Pegok, said, "No, really. This girl is the daughter of a holy man. She's ... she's ... It's hard to describe. It's like she doesn't need anything."

"Oh, my babies," said Wayan Buyar, "there's no such thing as a woman who doesn't need everything."

"Go get her, b'li," said the youngest, steering his sincerity toward his fat patron.

"Ah!" said Wayan Buyar. "So you do feel a tremor of fellow-feeling after all. Good for you, you small piece of shit. You may come out with me tonight."

"To her rescue!" said another, quick to read the weather.

"Save her from a life of deprivation!"

"Indeed. Yes ... A girl shielded from the world. We'll bring the world to her, wrapped in silver. Yes! An unspoiled vessel for the spoils of a man's spoiling."

"You're drooling," said the one who had been asleep.

"Is that your face or your bottom?" said Wayan Buyar. "I forget which is which." The young men responded with a round of farts and belches.

"Anyway," resumed Buyar, "you are all with me, I know. We leave in three days' time. What's the girl's name and where does she live?"

"Kusuma Sari. Gunung Kawi."

"Excellent address!"

"Gunung Kawi?" Gdé Kedampal disliked being disturbed while he was doing his accounts, but he so doted on his son that he was pleased to be interrupted by his visit. "Gunung Kawi — that's rather lofty for your taste, Wayan."

"I understand what you mean, sire," said Wayan Buyar, who was tucked contritely at his father's feet. This affected manner of his son both flattered and embarrassed the great man. "You are thinking of the spoiled sluts who so ungratefully milked us of our family riches before deserting their sacred duty."

"I'm thinking of your succession of disappointed wives, yes."

"Monkeys! Monkeys who thought they could pass for human beings the moment they put on their first pair of Italian shoes."

"They looked quite human, I thought, in shoes. Of course, shoes go right to the head with women, somehow. You're too generous with women, Wayan. What they really want from a husband is instruction. Nothing wins the heart of a woman like instruction."

"My devoted father," said Buyar, bowing his head behind raised hands. "This is surely a girl I can mold into a fine wife. Help me, Father, to win her."

Gdé Kedampal grinned and bid Wayan Buyar rise and sit next to him. He dropped his hand to his son's knee and wagged it slowly. "Now tell me what's on your mind, you puppy. What have you sniffed out at Gunung Kawi? Who's the little songbird this time?"

Several hours later, Wayan Buyar left his father's quarters slightly drunk and significantly heavier for the amount of silver he was carrying — most of it in coin, but some in the form of tiny flowers and fantastical animals, toys that his mother had brought with her as a bride. Wayan Buyar had convinced his father that he'd found a woman worthy of his dead mother's treasures.

Three days later, Wayan Buyar set out for Gunung Kawi with his band of followers, laden with silver and an assortment of gifts he was sure would win the heart of Kusuma Sari: fighting cocks, sunglasses, a poster of a film star ("Mountain girls like that sort of trashy stuff to put on the walls of their huts," explained Wayan Buyar, who himself kept posters of weightlifters on his walls.) They traveled on horses, and it is told that they raced them dangerously, galloping two and three abreast down village streets and trampling rice fields.

In this way, they quickly arrived at their destination.

It was morning on Gunung Kawi. Kusuma Sari was in the kitchen, and within the stillness of the house temple, Dukuh Siladri was deep in prayer. His soul rose and mingled with the smoke of the kitchen fire and with the bees of the orchard, and all about Gunung Kawi a song was moving through the trees, carried on firepoints at the tips of the coat of the tiger, and in tiny spheres of green and violet light hiding in the leaves of ground orchids. The song trailed over moss on the courtyard walls, billowed through fields of awakening grasses, and lifted up into the wide sky on the prayers of Dukuh Siladri.

Wild birds flashed in the forest, while in the orchard, surrounded by a swarm of bees, Mudita was helping to cross-pollinate the blossoms. The queen bee was curled on a flower tucked behind his ear, murmuring to him what she knew of the secrets of love:

> What a woman wants in love, Mudita
> Is to stand tall and free in her love, Mudita,
> And to find her husband's face above.

Kusuma Sari moved quickly about the courtyard, almost dancing between the kitchen and the other buildings, restoring order to the house. On the fire, big pots of rice and roots were steaming, and small pans of nuts and spices were frying. In a dark corner of the kitchen, the water jug stood full and cold; the floors were swept, and the hens had been fed and let out into the garden.

Kusuma Sari opened the sleeping rooms, chased away the night mustiness, and pulled the mats into the sun. A young male monkey accompanied her, tending to his cuticles from time to time. She gathered the sleeping clothes in a basket and set off again for the river gorge, and when she returned, her hair was wet and all the clothes had been washed and wrung into hard, cold knots. She spread them in the grass beyond the gate and shook out her hair to dry in the sun. High above, she saw the air quivering with the conversation between Mudita and the queen bee, laced with the praying of their father.

Far below, the ground was drumming with the galloping of horses. Visitors: a company of men. Kusuma Sari tied up her hair and walked back to the house, and the monkey took off on a diagonal canter toward the orchard.

Mudita saw the visitors arrive; he had come into the courtyard through the back gate, dusted with pollen. Kusuma Sari giggled when she saw him walking toward the kitchen.

"This morning you were more sweet than anything on earth, and now you are even sweeter still," she said. "Are you trying to send us to heaven?"

"Yes, as slowly as possible, like ants drowning in honey."

"Mudita, quickly, kiss me slowly just once — we have guests."

"I cannot kiss you only once."

"Then I will kiss you once. There. And once again. You see? It's very easy. Once. And again, once only. Mmmm, we must try this again tonight. And now I should see to our visitors. Oh, my perfect brother, you're covered in pollen. I will greet them while you wash your face. There must be at least ten of them. They look like they expect lots of the best of everything." The monkey suddenly swung down on to Kusuma Sari's shoulder and clung to her neck.

"And now you," she said. "If you don't climb down, you will have to greet them all. Jump!" The monkey only wrapped himself tighter around Kusuma Sari. "Come with me, then, little bones. But no crying or stealing — these are guests!"

Kusuma Sari walked toward the front courtyard, wrapped in a monkey whose eyes were as still as two yellow lamps.

Wayan Buyar posed in the center of the courtyard with seven of his minions arranged behind him, the other two having been commanded to guard the horses and gifts before the gate. Kusuma Sari approached them with her hands pressed politely in front of her chin.

"Good morning to you, gentlemen, and please be welcome here."

The dour-faced young man named Pegok returned her greeting. "And good morning to you, Miss. Would this be the house of Dukuh Siladri?"

"It is, sir."

"May I announce Wayan Buyar from Tumbensugih on urgent business with the Dukuh."

"Indeed, sir. Please come sit in the shade. My father is still at his prayers, but if you would kindly wait and rest a short while, he will join you soon."

Kusuma Sari steered the company to an elegant little pavilion and excused herself with a small bow.

"Delicious," said Wayan Buyar to Pegok. "She is already mine. Did you see how she pretended not to notice me?"

"She's certainly old-fashioned."

Kusuma Sari waited for Siladri to finish his prayers. "Father, we have guests. Men on horses."

"Horses, you say? Oh dear."

When Wayan Buyar saw Kusuma Sari return with the Dukuh, he stood up and coughed hard four or five times and then made a big show of clearing his lungs of a substantial amount of something from which Kusuma Sari averted her eyes.

"Greetings, teacher. I am Wayan Buyar, son of the unusually rich Gdé Kedampal of Tumbensugih."

"Welcome, sir. My name is Siladri. We are honored by your visit. It's a long way for you to come. Please sit down."

Wayan Buyar sat next to Dukuh Siladri, and his followers arranged themselves on the steps below.

"Oh, it's not far when you've got ten good horses," said Wayan Buyar. "We left only this morning." He helped himself to a cigarette from the little table between them.

"Then you must spend the night with us and rest," said Dukuh Siladri. The followers of Wayan Buyar nudged each other, and Wayan Buyar gave one of them a little kick in the back.

Kusuma Sari arrived with a tray of coffee and fruit.

"Tell me, teacher, is this beautiful girl your daughter?" said Wayan Buyar.

"Yes, this is Kusuma Sari." As he said this, Siladri was stung by the memory of Kadek saying these same words, so many years ago on their journey to Gunung Kawi. Now Kadek and even Mpu Dibiaja were part of the wind. He thought: I know we must all die many times, but this life seems to go on forever — but what he said was, "Sari, bring some more cigarettes for our guests. And now tell me, sir, what brings you so far, and so urgently?"

Wayan Buyar tucked up one leg and leaned confidentially toward Siladri. "Good news, teacher. Good news for you and good news for your little girl. Let me come right to the point. I am a very rich young man."

"How fortunate for you. Oh, thank you, Sari, and please ask Mudita to join us. As you were saying, sir."

"Right. I am a young man of fabulous wealth, and one day I hope to inherit a great deal more. You must have heard of my father, the great Gdé Kedampal."

"I have not — but I wish him a long life of good health."

"Oh, he's very healthy. As I was saying, I am very rich. And unmarried."

"Indeed?" said Siladri. He looked at his coffee and said mildly, "I myself am a widower."

Wayan Buyar rolled on. "And although I wouldn't be so boastful as to call myself handsome, I am attractive to women and considered brilliant."

"Is that so? Ah, Mudita. May I present to you, sir, my son."

Wayan Buyar glanced at Mudita and gave a short nod, then continued. "Many women have pursued me — princesses, the daughters of great traders — many have aspired to be the wife of Wayan Buyar. But I would have none of them."

His friend Pegok yawned loudly.

"Pardon the rude manners of my groom, teacher," said Wayan Buyar. "The journey has tired him out, although I myself feel as fresh as a flower. And so I should, for I am in excellent physical condition. In fact, I've often been told that I'm tireless!" Here he gave Dukuh Siladri a broad wink.

"You are blessed with much good fortune, sir," said Siladri, stifling a yawn.

"Exactly! A young man with riches, charm, and vigor would surely make a perfect husband. But I have been saving myself so that I may bestow all this upon a girl of purity and character. A girl such as your daughter."

"What!" said Mudita, leaping to a half-crouch. Then, seeing his father give him an almost imperceptible wink, he sat down quickly.

"Here is my proposal," said Wayan Buyar. He paused and turned to his friend. "'Gok, go get the presents," then continued. "Venerable teacher — may I call you 'Father'? — I should like to offer you the very generous sum of seven thousand silver ringgits if you will give me the hand of your daughter in marriage."

"What a great deal of money," said Dukuh Siladri.

"Yes, it is," said Wayan Buyar, "but I can see that she's an exceptional creature. I'm considered a good judge of women, you know. Now think, Father, what you could do with seven thousand solid silver ringgits. You could make this place very comfortable. And Kusuma Sari would be very happy with me, I can promise you that: my father is very, very rich."

Wayan Buyar drew out the silver from his purse and laid it on the table between them. "Now, what do you think of this? Feel it — real silver!"

Mudita and Kusuma Sari giggled behind their hands. Siladri silenced them with a frown and then looked at Wayan Buyar, who was leaning back with a fat smile on his face, displaying his awful teeth.

"Your offer is, as you say, very generous, sir," said Siladri, "but I'm sorry to disappoint you. Kusuma Sari is already married to her cousin — my son Mudita."

Just at that moment, Pegok returned with an armload of presents.

"She's what?" said Wayan Buyar. His features revolved involuntarily. He tried to smile but was hideously unsuccessful.

"Kusuma Sari is mine," said Mudita, jumping to his feet. Pegok erupted in a fit of giggling, and a movie poster slipped to the ground, making him laugh that much harder. Wayan Buyar let out a great howl, kicked over the little table of coffee, fruit, and silver, and lunged for Mudita, digging his fat fingers into Mudita's face. Mudita gave Wayan Buyar a mighty shove and sent him hurtling backward. Buyar bounced hard on his rump, but he leapt up and grabbed Kusuma Sari around the neck.

"I'll take the girl," he snarled to his followers. "You finish off the old man and his pansy of a son, and then come with me."

Mudita hurled himself at Wayan Buyar. Four of the thugs dragged him off Buyar and began to beat him; three more jerked Dukuh Siladri to his feet. Kusuma Sari let out a scream so piercing that for a few seconds everyone was paralyzed. Then one of the men snatched off the old man's headcloth and yanked him backward by his long gray hair. Another held his arms; a third drew a kris.

At that moment there was a ground-shaking roar, and the huge and furious weight of the old tiger felled the young man with the kris. Within an instant the assailant was nothing more than a pile of bloody clothes. The others began to flee in horror, crying and vomiting. Mudita ran after them with the fallen kris.

Wayan Buyar, his chin wet with slobber, kept hauling Kusuma Sari toward the gate; she didn't struggle, but let loose another terrible scream. In a streak of fur, the monkey landed on Wayan Buyar's neck and sank his fangs into the oily flesh. Kusuma Sari sprang free and raced to her father while Mudita leapt to the top of the wall just in time to see the forest animals swarming down on Wayan Buyar and his company. Eight of the horses had already fled, and the young men raced toward the remaining two. Wayan Buyar pulled one of his flunkies off the nearer horse and struggled into the saddle. Pegok was already galloping away under a barrage of wasps. Wild pigs were trampling three others into the ground. The youngest, the one Wayan Buyar always called "little shit", had scrambled up a tree to escape the charge of the lioness (Kusuma Sari's dam) only to be seized by a band of monkeys, who were now feasting on his innards.

The remaining three raced off into the forest, where they each quickly met their end: one by the lioness, another pierced and trampled by a stag, and the last, who tripped and fell against a rock and swooned unconscious, devoured in the night by ants.

Wayan Buyar and Pegok galloped toward the plains in the southwest. When at last they were among villages again, it was dark and they began to look for shelter.

"Did you remember to pick up the silver?" said Pegok.

"Of course I did. You don't think I panicked, do you?"

In one village they found an old soup seller who was still open. Inside the little hut, the lamplight was faint, but it couldn't hide the disarray of the two travelers. The other customers made way for the newcomers and waited curiously in the shadows.

The soup seller was a worn-out-looking woman, and she paid no attention to the dog poking around the soup pot on the ground.

"Are you traveling far tonight?" she said.

"As far from Gunung Kawi as possible," said Wayan Buyar.

"Gunung Kawi?" she said.

"Evil fucking place," said Pegok, whose face was hideous with welts. "That old man is a fucking witch."

"Witch?" said the soup seller. The other customers murmured among themselves.

Wayan Buyar lowered his voice. "This calls for professional help," he said to Pegok. "I'll have that girl if it costs my father everything he owns."

The soup seller kicked the dog away from the soup pot. She said to them, "Are you looking for someone?"

Wayan Buyar and Pegok exchanged glances.

"Do you know someone?" said Pegok, curling his fingers over his mouth.

The soup seller stared at them from under a cocked eyebrow.

"You could ask at Gunung Mumbul," said one of the customers from the shadows.

"Gunung Mumbul?" said Pegok.

"At the big house," continued the customer.

"Who do we ask for?" said Pegok. The customer glanced at the soup seller. The soup seller gave a little nod and turned away.

"Ask for Dayu Datu."

Wayan Buyar and Pegok spent an uncomfortable night in the community pavilion of the village. Wayan Buyar's neck swelled with a smelly wound where the monkey had bitten him, and Pegok blubbered in pain from his stings, a pain that grew hotter with every moment. The stone floor of the hall was cold and filthy, and mosquitoes annoyed the travelers' ears and stung their fingers. As soon as the night began to fade, the two men set off for Gunung Mumbul.

They headed for the low dark hills in the southwest. As the day grew hot, the ground became marshy, even as it rose, and there was a sulfurous odor in the mud. The horses became irritable. The vegetation was thick with low scrub, making it impossible to proceed any faster than a stumbling trot. Thorny bushes scratched open the skin of the horses' chests and bellies, and big flies flew drunkenly about their heads. There was no sign of human habitation.

Wayan Buyar and Pegok were thirsty and dirty, their bodies hurt, and their wounds were more painful than ever. They scratched at the mosquito bites on their hands, cursed the landscape, beat their horses futilely on their heads and flanks, and still the hills seemed to come no nearer.

"You're a fucking idiot, 'Gok. Can't you find a path through this ugly country?"

"*You* find a path, Buyar. This is your fucking love quest."

Dayu Datu smiled as she watched the two travelers from a light trance. It amused her to irritate visitors as they approached, but her real reason for doing so was practical: if clients arrived in ill temper, they were more likely to settle their business quickly and be off. Dayu Datu disliked company, and she did not entertain.

In time Wayan Buyar and Pegok found themselves in the shadow of a high wall with a noble gate.

"Do you think this is it?" said Wayan Buyar.

"I don't care whose house it is. I'm not leaving until I feel better. In fact, I don't care if you have to buy the place, I want some coffee."

They walked through the gate and entered a broad courtyard. There were ornate pavilions all around, and everywhere they saw young women in colorful brocade and heavy gold jewelry.

"I think we've come to the right place," said Pegok. "One could easily forget about that farm girl from the mountains. What do you think?"

"I will have her," said Wayan Buyar, "and I will dress her in the skins of her murderous father and cousin. Now shut up and go announce me."

Dayu Datu received her visitors in her office. It was, for this occasion, a tiny concrete cubicle with no other furniture than a large desk on a dais with a high-backed leather chair, where Dayu Datu sat swiveling back and forth and gazing at the ceiling while Wayan Buyar presented his situation.

He began like this: "Good morning, my lady. I am Wayan Buyar of Tumbensugih, son of the great lord Gdé Kedampal."

"Not a lord, I think." Dayu Datu's thin lips unpeeled her words as she spoke. "What do you want?"

"I would like your help, madam. To kill a witch."

Dayu Datu sighed, took a pad of paper from a drawer, and pulled a ballpoint pen from behind her ear. "What's the name of the witch?" she said, not looking at either of them.

"He's called Dukuh Siladri."

"Locality of practice?"

"Gunung Kawi, my lady. Perhaps I should give you some details on the nature of my case. You see, he is holding my wife captive. The real villain is his son Mudita, an arrogant and sadistic criminal, a known murderer. Only yesterday he abducted my wife and abused her in a most unspeakable way. I, with the help of my manservant here, fought gallantly with my bare hands and surely would have finished him off myself with no difficulty at all. But then his father — posing as a holy man, no less! — transformed himself into a horrible tiger and attacked us, which accounts for our rather disheveled appearance. Of course I killed the tiger, but you know how it is with witches: the next moment a swarm of enchanted animals was pursuing us, and although I managed to kill most of them, that witch Siladri is still alive and my poor wife is imprisoned there. When I think of what that snake Mudita must be doing to her I become, I confess, nearly mad with grief."

Wayan Buyar here choked up a few tears, but Dayu Datu simply drummed her fingernails on the desk. "Get to the point."

"This Siladri is a most evil imposter. My lady, I'm prepared to offer you one thousand solid silver ringgits for the death of this monster and his villainous son. I consider it my public duty. With, of course, the return of my wife included."

"Four thousand silver ringgits, and the wife will be another three."

"Four thousand — with the wife," Wayan Buyar countered.

"I do not bargain."

"Oh. Well, yes, as you prefer. Seven thousand."

"In advance."

"Ah. In advance ..." Wayan Buyar mumbled.

"If you cannot pay this now, please go away."

"No, no, it's no trouble at all. Perhaps you would agree to half in advance and the other half on delivery?"

"No."

"I understand. Well, in that case, I feel that I must insist on a discount if I am to pay such a sum in cash."

"Get out."

"My lady, let us settle the matter now, shall we? Seven thousand ringgits, then. Here you are, madam. Seven thousand in coin and ... figurines of unsurpassed craftsmanship, certainly worth more than —"

Dayu Datu sliced his words with a gaze, her eyes like slits of dry ice. Wayan Buyar laid the silver on the desk, and in anticipation of the trays of refreshments that would be brought by the women in brocade, he rubbed his hands together and said, "And now —"

Dayu Datu smiled through her teeth. "Thank you. Goodbye."

A moment later, the two men found themselves once more struggling through the marshy scrub. Wayan Buyar said, "Well, she's very professional, I think. You have to know how to talk to them, of course. Did you notice how well I presented the case?"

"I didn't notice that she gave you a receipt," said Pegok.

"She'll give me more than a receipt," said Wayan Buyar. "Perfect satisfaction is very near at hand."

Dayu Datu sat alone in her office.

Outside, the midday sun was bleaching out the colors of the day. Her students moved in twos and threes across the courtyard, much as girls in broad spaces do everywhere, except that some were walking on their hands and rolling balls of fire with their feet. Dayu Datu sat very still. Then she murmured, "Somebody bring me Klinyar."

A moment later, Klinyar walked in and closed the door.

She was a beautiful girl, small and neatly shaped, and she had a tendency to turn pale gold at midday. Dayu Datu greeted her with warm dark eyes. "Klinyar, I have some work for you. Tonight I want you to go to Gunung Kawi and see all that there is to see of the house of Dukuh Siladri. Go in the guise of a bird and be back by tomorrow afternoon."

Klinyar curtsied.

"I have heard that Siladri may be a witch," said Dayu Datu. "Be careful."

JUST AFTER DARK, Klinyar steeped herself in trance and shivered into the form of a shiny black bird. She arched her shoulders, then spread her arms and stretched her fingers, and springing up on her toes, she lifted herself and flew off into the night.

Klinyar ducked through the branches of the forest, past the highest treetops, and broke into the clear wide night sky. Splendid bowl of night! Did she feel the same rush of cinnamon and diamonds that her mother had felt on the night of Klinyar's conception? Klinyar sucked in the cold air through her beak and soared in a deep figure eight. She beat her way upward toward the stars until her heart began to knock, and then she glided in a slow spiral toward the northeast.

Before long, the mountain of Gunung Kawi appeared in the distance, rising pale and luminous in the night air. Klinyar swooped down toward the forest and planed in a wide circle around the entire mountain. With her sharp bird's eyes, she could see fireflies glinting through the trees. Klinyar dropped lower and scanned the forest. She looked high on the mountain slopes and low in the foothills. In the moonlight she saw fields and groves and thick rain forest, but nowhere could she see any sign of a house, not even a farmer's hut.

All night Klinyar searched Gunung Kawi, but she could not find the house of Dukuh Siladri. Finally the sky lost its black luster, and dawn began to scroll up from the east. Klinyar fluttered down into a river gorge and landed with a little hop on the bank of the stream. Still in her bird feet, she strutted up and down the stream for a few minutes and caught a crayfish for breakfast. But dawn had broken and so had Klinyar's spell: feathers mutated back into her natural girl-shape, dressed in rich brocade. The crayfish wriggled and scratched her throat. Klinyar gave a hearty Balinese cough, cleared her throat, and began to undress. It was morning; she would bathe.

And now Klinyar, for the first time in her life, was in a moment entirely private. She slithered out of her clothes, across the sunlight, and into the stream, and sat down in the water, letting her legs float before her, counting the vertebrae as the cold rose up her spine. She rolled over and floated downstream for a while, face-down in the water, and watched the fish. She spread the soles of her feet to the sun and felt as vivid and stupid and translucent as the fish. The river moved through her hair, the sandy bottom pinged against her belly and cat-like nipples.

The stream was glittering and cold, and the sun was lighting up the highest trees at the top of the gorge. Klinyar angled her face to pull the sunlight down into her features and then flipped over quickly, dipping her face again in the stream to quiet her smiling. A swell of electricity moved over her, wavy like a signature. She felt: I am this, Klinyar, down at the river at daybreak. I must be at the very center of the world.

For almost an hour Klinyar rolled and played in the stream, as mindless as moss, jabbering with the water and the filaments of thistles. She poked up her back in fins; she raised her belly in a wreath of dead leaves; she burrowed under the mud and let her eyes become the eggs of turtles. The day, meanwhile, slid down the ravine.

Klinyar finally grew bored with her bath. She sat and threw rocks at a nest of kingfishers for a while, and then stood up.

Klinyar rubbed her face and pulled the water back from her hair. Crossing her arms from the cold, she walked teeter-tottering to the bank of the stream. Her arms were aching and icy as she picked up her sarong and wrapped it around her hips. Her fingers were stiff as she wound her breast cloth around and around, across her belly and up under her arms, enclosing her torso in that neat cocoon peculiar to young Balinese girls. She picked up her gilded leather collar and tied it around her neck, and was just fastening her bracelets when she heard a sound coming from the other side of the gorge. She froze in violet rock shadow and let her eyes slide to the opposite bank.

First there was the sound of singing, but richer and deeper than any singing that Klinyar had ever heard. It was a bursting forward kind of song, dangerous and warm. And then it appeared. It was a man.

Mudita had come down to the river to bathe. She hurriedly undressed again.

Klinyar unwound her sarong in the shadow of the rock, and in a moment she was crouching naked in the stream, her arms pumping fiercely as she labored away at the washing of her clothes. But one detail flawed her performance, and perhaps it was this that led to the extraordinary consequences that soon followed: Klinyar, in her distraction, had neglected to take hold of her real clothes, and what Mudita saw when he arrived on the opposite side of the stream was a naked girl performing a pantomime of laundering.

This apparition stunned him.

He was shocked to see anyone at all at his normal bathing place. Although he had bathed here with Kusuma Sari in the early months of their marriage, they had each drifted into individual morning rhythms, as married people do, becoming distinct and interlocking in their private routines, like the fingers of right hand and left. Indeed, Mudita had come to savor this time at the beginning of each day. It was here at the river, after his bath, that he carried out his morning prayers, not wanting to disrupt the rituals of his father in the nexus of the house temple, nor Kusuma Sari in her devotions between the water jug and the hearth. For Mudita, daybreak at the river was the time and place in which he came back to the root of himself.

Also, he was shocked by the beauty of the girl.

She was daintier than Kusuma Sari. Even from the far side of the riverbank, he could see the translucence of her ears, and even though her back was turned he could make out the dark pulsing of her heart deep within her rib cage. He was puzzled and a little dizzied by the opalescence that swirled over her skin, and it seemed to him that her long hair was crawling like a nest of snakes viewed through a deep pool.

Finally he was struck with grief to see that this exquisite stray was a poor mad girl, whacking away at her imaginary washing. He stood there rock still and waited to see what would happen.

Klinyar let her eyes sink into slits as she continued her pantomime. She had made a technical error and recognized it almost immediately, but her artfulness knew this to be but a fractal event on which fresh mystery could be composed. She let slip a neat ellipsis of time during which her features and the points of her ears moved slightly toward the back of her head.

"Who's this?" she said. It wasn't clear whether she meant Mudita or herself.

Without touching him, without even looking at him, the girl tugged at Mudita. And yet something icy, deep in his skull, told him that he was in the presence of an evil that pulsated far beyond that sun-dappled ravine. The danger had a metallic taste and seemed to point toward his home — at his father, his precious wife, and his galloping heart.

"You," said Klinyar. "Come here and help me, please!"

She was struggling now with an imaginary load, and as he walked into the water, it only grew wider and deeper. And now he was confused. The stream should not be so high. It was a dry time of the year. It was, in fact, Sasih Kapat, exactly one year from the time he had first set out to find his father on Gunung Kawi, and yet this stream that normally reached only to his knees was rushing against his hips, and now his belly, and now almost freezing his liver, spleen, and heart. He raised his arms and struggled forward. And then the ground began to rise. He approached the other bank and the multicolored girl squatting in the shallows. Mudita, too, crouched.

He addressed the girl politely. "Where do you come from, little sister?"

Klinyar smiled over her invisible laundry.

He tried again. "Do you live around here?" He would have to return the girl to her family, and thus was glad see a pile of real clothes on the riverbank. "What is your father's name?"

Klinyar's mind whipped around the page of circumstance on which she found herself. Taking a chance and trying to think of a sewing needle, she said, "I'm sorry. I'm lost."

Mudita's heart was bouncing. A ripple of vermilion flashed over the spine of Klinyar. She thought, this is real magic. Inspired, she lifted both wrists and held her hands limp before her face. She let her mouth fall open in a little oval and she said, "Help me lift this heavy load of washing."

"Of course, of course," said Mudita. His heart was breaking like an egg: she was so young, so fragile, this lost girl naked and hallucinating at the bottom of a river gorge, and her little mouth was so like the insides of a pretty fish.

"Please, help me lift this," she said. She stood up and Mudita stood up quickly, too, and pretended to take hold of something heavy somewhere near her hands — beautiful hands, as fine as script.

"Not like that," said Klinyar. "Just lift it up and put it on my head!" The pantomime was very clumsy, and it allowed Klinyar to bump up against Mudita.

The top of Klinyar's head came just to the middle of Mudita's breastbone. Her ear was even with his heart, and her arms rose and timidly encircled Mudita's waist.

Poor, gentle Mudita! Deadly, birdlike Klinyar! The morning was empty all around them, and there was no sound but the rushing water. Mudita felt his body going awry. His heart and face churned with the sensation of sobbing, his arms closed around Klinyar, and deep between his buttocks there grew the most urgent inquisitiveness.

As for Klinyar, she felt swept up in some entirely new physical music. This big sweet-smelling brotherly creature in her arms, who sheltered her head and her left shoulder with his hand, who shivered when she shivered, this emerging lover, was a flavor for which Klinyar had not been prepared. She let her knees buckle and her eyes roll back and her lips tug forward and smear against the perfect belly of Mudita. Mudita felt as if his head were lifting into the sky. They ground their feet against the creeping sand at the bottom of the stream. They staked themselves more firmly against each other, stiff against the current, and entwined, ever closer, ever better, until in a soft explosion they were suddenly and frantically deep inside each other, all pumping and suction.

It was then that Kusuma Sari appeared at the riverbank.

Kusuma sari came down to the river and saw Mudita swaying in the current with a strange girl. She saw his eyes rolled back and his head tilted slightly as if he were listening to something far away. She saw the strange girl clasping Mudita as she herself did, but the girl's arms were paler than her own, and slimmer, and they didn't belong there.

In the still morning darkness, Kusuma Sari had sniffed his lips in her sleep, and later, at first light, she had awakened in the full bloom of craving. Arching her back, she had reached for Mudita, but he had gone, already risen. She had rushed through her earliest chores with a thick little smile on her face at the thought of surprising him, naked at the river, as they had been naked there together in the rainy season.

Swollen with happiness, humming with love, she had come looking for Mudita, only to find him bucking in the embrace of another girl, flailing in the river, laying waste to her world. Kusuma Sari stared and felt as though her skin had split open. She stretched out her arm: a big stick leapt into her hand, and she charged across the river. Her feet did not even touch the water.

Kusuma Sari began shrieking the moment she stretched out her arm. The stick that leapt into her hand had been, an instant before, a quiet brown snake. Now she held a hard, heavy staff, and she struck and struck at the copulating pair until they broke apart. Then she struck at Mudita as if she could beat him back into the man he had been in that morning dark. He fled to the riverbank, weeping, his face mottled as if with measles.

Kusuma Sari turned and began to beat her rival, but Klinyar jumped out of reach, bristling with spangles of gold and screaming a ribbon of the vilest obscenity. Kusuma Sari flew at her, scratching and kicking, knocked her to the ground, and heard the sand grind against Klinyar's flesh. Grabbing a handful of snaking hair, she said, "Who are you, and where do you come from, slut?"

"Oh, indeed. I am Ni Klinyar from the palace of Dayu Datu. And get off me, cow bag! I can turn you into a little smear of dog shit on your kitchen door."

"A witch, is it? A piece of tinsel that can say its prayers upside down?"

Kusuma Sari grinned at Klinyar and yanked her head back. In the river gorge, a soft wind rattled the leaves of the coconut palms high overhead.

Klinyar turned a muddy orange, and then she hissed and slithered out of Kusuma Sari's grasp. She stood up and pirouetted on the bank, flashing sparkles in the morning air, and ripped the gorge with laughter that sounded like shattering glass.

"Lick my beautiful feet!" Klinyar sang out.

Pointing her stick at Klinyar, Kusuma Sari spoke in the cadence of magical curses. It was the sound of a young girl's voice coming from a stone. It was a sound that made Mudita feel cold and sick.

"Ni Klinyar," she groaned in her strange and dangerous voice, "you are nobody. Be quiet."

"How-dare-you-speak-down-to-me!"

Mudita crouched at the far end of the riverbank, his lips growing numb. "Sari, be careful!"

Kusuma Sari, still pointing, advanced toward Klinyar, muttering, "Snail slime, neck grease, dead rot, fall in your tracks!"

A bolt of fire shot from the top of Klinyar's head as she went into trance and then jellied into the form of a hideous wild pig.

The details were immaculate: her little tail switched at a cloud of cholera-laden flies; her eyes were topaz beads and gummy at the corners; the stiff hairs growing from her snout were encrusted with the excrement of picnickers. Her wild pig was, moreover, a furious male of supernatural size with a heavy, bludgeon-like head and testicles burning with eczema. The monster cantered this way and that on the tiny beach, its hooves plowing deep, flinging wet sand into Kusuma Sari's face. It threw its head about, rolling its eyes like marbles, and grunted filthily to itself. All the while it gave off a smoky fire from its ears and mouth and anus that stung the eyes of Mudita and Kusuma Sari and made them bite their lips to keep from vomiting.

The unholy boar swung its head along a low axis and fixed its sights, then plunged like a bomber toward Mudita. He scrambled up the bank, and the boar cantered in an ugly little circle.

Kusuma Sari kept her eyes on the boar. "Mudita," she said in a voice low and dull like the cracking of river rocks, "you will not leave."

"It will kill us! Come home, Sari, come on!"

"No." Droning now, she intoned, "Don't ask me to be frightened with you. If it's time for us to die, we'll die. Hiding in the kitchen won't save us. Stay with me, husband."

Mudita turned and faced the magical boar.

It stopped in its tracks.

And now Kusuma Sari stepped between them. Facing the monster, she said, almost growling, "Look. It's just a pig. Skillful, Klinyar, but look at you: just a pig. Wouldn't you rather be a human being? Hmmm? Rather than a wild animal that eats its own shit?"

The boar lowered its ugly head, gave a short snort of fire, and trotted in place as it prepared to charge.

Kusuma Sari knelt in front of it and said, "All right, then. I'll fight you." She gathered herself into trance and lifted her right hand slightly. A rose appeared in her fingers and she held it to her heart, awakening the flower with mantras. A wonderful smell of blossoms filled the air. And then Kusuma Sari flicked the rose at the boar.

Flames burst from the rose and landed like fire bolts on the pig, searing it, and in an instant the boar was gone. There was only Klinyar, badly scorched and racing up the river bank.

But then she stopped and came back and stood in front of Kusuma Sari.

Suddenly Mudita and Kusuma Sari were knocked to the ground by the resplendent vision called Suku Tunggal Chandra Berawa Luwih Sakti — the Moon with Rings Fabulously Dangerous.

"Oh you're very mighty, Klinyar," said Kusuma Sari. She rose up and became the vision called the Dangerous Moon Pierced by Fire, swelling into a vast inferno until the Moon with Rings was consumed and Klinyar lay cursing at the edge of the water.

Then Klinyar curled her soul in upon herself until it became as hard and brilliant as a diamond. From the farthest reaches of the netherworld she summoned the god Brahma Semeru, and there erupted before Kusuma Sari and Mudita a cataclysmic monster with a thousand heads, its body boiling with fire. A mountain of oily smoke darkened the gorge.

Streaming with fear, Mudita groped for his wife. "Sari, please, let's go," he moaned. "This is a very powerful witch."

"Shut up."

Again Kusuma Sari went into trance. She called on the highest lords of heaven, and in a convulsion of sound and thermal fury she became the vision called Amurti Sanghyang Ongkara Wisnu Sakti, the Three in One. Mudita swooned. Kusuma Sari raised the frequency of her radiation and became the Duality of Truth. Finally she summoned the Single Force of Shiva, and there burst forth an explosion of the Holy Weapons *bajera*, *dupa*, *danda*, *suduk*, *pasah*, *cakra*, *trisula*. They gleamed with holy terror and flew at the flaming many-headed fiend. With a terrible roar the apparition exploded, leaving only Klinyar sputtering and limp on the river bank, collapsed at the feet of Kusuma Sari.

"Get up," scolded Kusuma Sari. "Don't crawl so low on the ground. Look, you have sand all over your face. Come, stand up."

She helped Klinyar to her feet and perfunctorily brushed the sand from her. Mudita stood up and walked over to the two witches, now girls again. His legs wobbled and his heart felt like a carcass. He spoke first to his wife. "I don't know which is greater, my shame or my love."

Kusuma Sari saw that he was indeed the same sweet brother she had sniffed that morning and had loved from the first moment she saw him. She filled her eyes with him and smiled.

Then Mudita said, "Klinyar, I'm sorry. It may be that you tricked me, but still you are a girl, and I'm sorry that I have spoiled you and cannot take care of you. I love only Kusuma Sari. But you are a pretty girl, and very clever and courageous, and I hope that you will find real love one day. Only please, don't practice black magic anymore. It can only bring you harm."

Kusuma Sari and Mudita gazed at Klinyar, sagging and expressionless. They saw the scorches on her face, arms, and legs; they noticed her leather collar torn and skewed by the heat of her magic.

Passing her perfumed hand over Klinyar's face and limbs, Kusuma Sari said, "And now be well, little artist. You are healed. Come now, stand up straight."

The sun was high in the sky now, lighting up the gorge. Klinyar stood between Mudita and Kusuma Sari, as limp as an empty silk purse.

Kusuma Sari turned Klinyar toward her and said, "You may go home. Go home to your parents, Klinyar. Don't return to Dayu Datu." She glanced briefly at Mudita, then continued. "You are a woman now. You're old enough to choose. Give up this religion of witchcraft and go home."

"And then?" said Siladri. "Did she agree?"

"Yes," said Kusuma Sari. "She said she would. I think she will. I think I have broken her."

"Dayu Datu," said Siladri. He gazed out over the trees. "If this young witch of yours was a protégée of Dayu Datu, then Dayu Datu must be quite a witch herself. And for some reason she is interested in us. My children, we must be alert. And Sari —" Siladri looked long and carefully at Kusuma Sari before going on. "That was a very impressive demonstration of your skill."

Alarmed, Kusuma Sari and Mudita looked at each other; they hadn't described Kusuma Sari's magic. They said only that she had managed to subdue Klinyar.

"May I ask you this," said Siladri. "Did you find that kind of magic ... exciting?"

"Exciting, sir?" said Kusuma Sari, puzzled.

"I hope that you did not. You have a fine pure heart, but you are also still very young. It would be dangerous if you forgot that such power is not one's own. It was good of you, and proper, to spare this girl's life and heal the injuries you caused her. It's fortunate that she wasn't killed. It would be a terrible sin for you to carry. Remember what our sainted teacher Dibiaja told us of *sakti*: it carries extraordinary consequences. I would not like it if you were to develop a taste for this sort of thing."

Kusuma Sari sat for a few minutes without saying a word, and then excused herself and went out into the garden. She walked past the ranks of long beans and beds of onions. As she passed a bush of marigolds, she plucked a blossom and rubbed it in her hands. She kept walking, washing her hands in its scent, and then her throat twisted up in a knot. Her grief mounting like panic, Kusuma Sari headed into the forest, in the direction of the river.

She passed Sang-Gadja-the-Elephant swaying in the sunlight, who saw her rushing by, but he said nothing. She startled a family of deer who bolted three steps, then turned and silently watched her go by. As she hurried down the side of the river gorge, she passed a huddle of young monkeys grooming each other's heads. They watched Kusuma Sari hurtle past, but they let her go without a greeting.

When she came to the river, Kusuma Sari saw the scarred bank on the other side, and her chest crushed in upon itself: hoof prints, scorched wood, and the smell of burnt flesh smeared the privacy of the place; a little gold earring glinted at the water's edge. She crossed the stream without removing her clothes, and when she came to the opposite bank, she did what any Balinese woman would do in the aftermath of a great event: she began to clean up.

She found a branch and swept away the footprints of battle. She found an ember of burning coconut husk, blew on it, and sprinkled it with dried leaves until her little fire was burning well. Upon that she placed every trace of bitten-off hide, shattered tusk, and wounded tree that she could find, and she nursed the fire with skill and prayerfulness until all traces of the magical war were cremated.

Then, still in her smoky clothes, Kusuma Sari washed herself in the river. When her skin was as cold and simple as the river rocks themselves, she moved upstream to the little spring. Breaking off a large yam leaf and folding it into a cone-shaped cup, she gathered spring water and held it above her head. She let the water pour in a stream over her head and down her breasts and back. She whispered mantras as she poured, and then gathered another leaf-cup of water and repeated this nine times. Ten times she cleansed herself, for the ten ills that afflict a human soul, then she tossed the leaf-cup into the stream and let it dart away.

Now purified to numbness, Kusuma Sari turned toward the riverbank and home. She wrung out her hair and looked around for her sandals. And then she noticed a cloudy presence perched on a rock nearby. It was Klinyar.

They looked at each other for a few moments, Kusuma Sari in surprise, Klinyar with opaline curiosity.

Finally Kusuma Sari said, "I'm glad you're still here, because there is one last thing I must do before I can go home and cook rice with a clear mind."

Klinyar stretched and popped her knuckles, but her face was stiff, and she only nodded. Kusuma Sari knelt before her. Putting her hands together in front of her face, she said, "Klinyar, earlier today, as surely as you wanted to kill me, I also wanted to kill you. Forgive me. Please."

Klinyar sat there for a moment, and finally she spoke. Her voice was low and scratchy. "I don't understand."

Kusuma Sari dropped her hands and sat back on her haunches.

"Come sit beside me," she said.

Klinyar hopped down and sat neatly beside Kusuma Sari on the riverbank. She noticed the bit of gold glinting in the water and felt her earlobe, but she did not retrieve the earring.

Kusuma Sari also looked at the earring. She said, "Klinyar, do you know who you are?"

Klinyar's body twitched and she flashed through a frightening display of color changes. "You told me — I'm nobody."

"You are Klinyar. Now, who is Klinyar?"

"I don't know. Tell me something else." Klinyar began to weep. "Now I'm lost in life."

Kusuma Sari watched the colors streaming through the girl. She stood up and said, "Is that your earring in the water?"

"Yes."

"Then pick it up and put it on," said Kusuma Sari, "and then forgive me."

Klinyar reached into the water and caught the little earring. As she fastened it to her ear, she glanced at Kusuma Sari. A little smile of embarrassment flitted across her face. Then, turning until she looked directly at Kusuma Sari, she said, "I forgive you."

"That's who you are — a pretty girl standing by the river between your own two earrings. You are Ni Klinyar, and you a human being, just like me and Mudita and, no doubt, Dayu Datu. You have a soul that is part of the world forever."

Klinyar stared at the ground and said with her lips, " 'I am all the world. And so are you.' " She looked up suddenly at Kusuma Sari. "Somebody said that to me once."

The two young women faced each other, marveling, silent. The stream beside them sparkled.

At last Klinyar said, "So that's it. We are all as grand as that." She stood simply, with her arms by her sides. Then the two girls tucked in their chins and laughed richly. Tears of relief sprang up in Kusuma Sari's eyes.

"Come home and have some rice," she said, the way she would have to a younger sister.

Klinyar took Kusuma Sari's hand and said, "Thank you. Perhaps one day I will, but now I will go home and see what's become of my parents." And then, not knowing how to say what she felt, she kissed the palm of Kusuma Sari's hand.

Kusuma Sari turned Klinyar's little hand in hers and returned the kiss. "Blessings on your life," she said, "and on your life forever after."

And so they parted, each on their separate ways, and each girl was changed. Returning home, Kusuma Sari vowed in her soul never again to practice sorcery — it was enough to be a human being. Klinyar, in her own way, mulled on the same thought. She had been defeated by a power that was divine, but the lesson had come from a girl.

Siladri, from his reading pavilion, surveyed all this and said to Mudita, whose hand he held, "Well, they've made their peace and that is good. There is no peace while women are at war. Now tell me, Mudita, aren't you troubled to have such a powerful wife?"

"Troubled?" Mudita's face brightened with amazement. "But why? Should a husband be troubled if his wife is beautiful and can do anything?"

Siladri closed his hand over Mudita's. "No, indeed. A man's wife is his ... what can one say? Like his house, but ever so much more wonderful. Like a magical friend. Your mother, Mudita, she was — she was like everything at once."

Father and son were quiet for several minutes.

"I only wonder," said Siladri, habitual wonderer that he was, "what will come next. I think our story is not yet finished."

ALL was waiting.

On Gunung Mumbul, Dayu Datu was waiting for Klinyar to return. In the village of Tumbensugih, Wayan Buyar was waiting for the delivery of Kusuma Sari and the heads of Dukuh Siladri and Mudita. And on Gunung Kawi, Siladri waited for the next assault from Dayu Datu.

When Wayan Buyar returned home from his adventure to Gunung Kawi — filthy and exhausted, with a wound on his neck bubbling with infection — Gdé Kedampal was frightened by the sight of his son.

"My darling boy, I've been so worried. What has happened to you?"

"Oh, fuck it!" said Wayan Buyar. He slid off his horse and limped to his pavilion without looking at his father.

Gdé Kedampal called for attendants to see to the comfort of his son, and sent a servant for the doctor. For the next week Wayan Buyar lay in a fever and could not be persuaded to speak to anyone, except to give orders to his attendants.

"Fan harder, you pig-faced idiot, can't you see I'm dying?"

"My lord, here is the iced melon juice you asked for. My wife has brought it all the way from Ubud."

"Take that mess away from my sight, the ice is half melted. What took her so long? She must have stopped fifty times along the road to sell her cunt."

"My lord, do take a little sip. It's still cold and you need refreshment."

"Give it to my dog."

Gdé Kedampal leaned over the bed and said softly, "Wayan, my child. Wayan, it's Papa."

Wayan Buyar moaned and rolled his eyes back until only the whites were visible through his fluttering lids. He raised his upper lip against his nostrils and made a thick clicking sound with his tongue against the roof of his mouth.

"Wayan ..."

" ... ehn ... nyeh ... eh ..."

"Oh, the poor boy," said Gdé Kedampal. He turned to the servant and said, "Can't you see he needs water? What's the matter with you, old man? He needs liquids, as much as he can drink, I made that very clear. Wayan ... Wayan?"

Gdé Kedampal doted perhaps unnecessarily on his son, but in the affairs of everyday life he was a man of action. The very evening of his son's return he summoned Pegok to recount what had happened. The interview was not a comfortable one.

Gdé Kedampal received the youth on the veranda of a grand pavilion. He was seated on an imposing chair, while Pegok was obliged to sit on the floor. He had never liked this boy who was Wayan Buyar's best friend; he seemed to him to be a sneaky and unsavory sort of person.

"Now, young man, I must tell you that I am distressed to see the condition in which my only child has returned from a journey on which you, I believe, were his chief companion."

Pegok sighed and said, "Yes, sir. We all had a pretty hard time of it, sir. The others didn't get away."

"My word! What happened, boy?"

"Well, sir. We got to Gunung Kawi in good time, sir, considering all that we had to carry. We found the house of this Dukuh Siladri. I never encouraged Wayan about this girl, sir. I didn't think she was his type, if you get my meaning, sir."

"No, I don't. What do you mean?"

"Well, sir. Her father is this *dukuh*, you see, very pious. No offense, sir. It's just that this girl is different from a town girl, if you see what I mean, sir."

"Go on. What happened when you got there?"

"They were all right to us at first. The old man was polite and all that, and the girl was, too. Wayan was having a good chat with the old man." Pegok paused and tried to remember just what happened next. "Then he made an offer for the girl. I went out to get the dough — uh, the gifts, that is, sir — and maybe I missed some of the conversation then, but what I caught was this girl is already married to her cousin, the old man's son."

Gdé Kedampal frowned and leaned forward. "Well? Then what?"

"Well, sir, you know Wayan. He sometimes has a bit of a temper."

"He's got a fiery character, yes, I'll grant that."

"Yes, sir. Well, a fight broke out between Wayan and this cousin of the girl, and the next thing we knew, the old man turned into a tiger and attacked us."

"What do you mean, he turned into a tiger? Are you telling me that Dukuh Siladri is a witch?"

"He sure as shit is. Sir. It was horrible. Everybody panicked and —"

"Is this when Wayan was wounded?"

"Yes, sir. And so was I — a whole cloud of wasps attacked me, sir. God, it was awful. And the others, I don't know what happened to them. We just tried to get away as fast as possible."

"And the horses? I sent you out with ten good horses."

"Well, we made it away with two, Wayan and me."

"You'll leave yours here, of course."

"Yes, sir. Of course, sir."

"And the silver?"

"The what, sir?"

"The silver, you pup! Wayan was carrying seven thousand silver ringgits and some very valuable silver figurines. What's become of the silver?"

"Oh, the *silver*." Pegok's eyes darted about. What was he supposed to say now? "Well, sir. I think he had already given the silver to the old man. That's right. He gave it to the old man and then the old man attacked us and we escaped."

Gdé Kedampal peered closed at Pegok. "Are you sure? These are serious charges. If we are to prosecute a witch for theft and assault and possibly murder, we must be very sure of our case. It will stand on your testimony, you realize. It could be very dangerous for you to annoy a witch with false charges. Think carefully, boy, and try to remember exactly what happened."

Pegok, now sweating disagreeably, put his fingers to his brow in the attitude of someone trying to think. "Ah, yes. It's coming back to me, sir. I remember now. I saved the silver."

"Indeed?" said Gdé Kedampal. "Good work. Now if you'll be good enough to return it to me, I don't think there's any reason to keep you here any longer."

"Oh, but sir. I don't have it."

"What's this? Certainly it wasn't in my son's luggage. Speak up, boy. If I catch you lying, you'll regret it for the rest of your life."

"Sir, I can explain!" Pegok was now quivering. He didn't owe Buyar anything, the arrogant idiot. He'd nearly been killed trying to help Buyar get this girl. "Here's what happened really, sir, and this is the truth."

"I should hope everything you're saying is truth, young man."

"Yes, sir. It is, sir. Well, we got away from that place as fast as we could and spent a miserable night in some village, I'm not sure exactly where, sir, but there were plenty of mosquitoes, so it was already somewhere in the south. We talked things over and decided that since this Siladri was obviously a witch, we'd better fight fire with fire, if you understand my meaning, sir."

"You engaged another sorcerer."

"Yes, sir. That's right, sir."

"And that's where the silver has gone?"

"Yes, sir."

Gdé Kedampal sighed heavily. "All of it?"

"Yes, sir. Wayan tried to bargain her down, but this was a pretty icy character."

"I see. I don't suppose you thought to ask for a receipt?"

"Uh, Wayan did all the negotiating, sir. I don't think he got a receipt, sir."

"Did you think to remark the sorcerer's name and address?"

Pegok opened his mouth to answer but found his jaws locked and his tongue frozen.

"Don't gape at me, boy! What's the witch's name?"

A choking sound came from Pegok's throat. He jumped up and then crouched on the ground and pounded the earth three times. "D-D-Dayu Datu," he spat out in a whisper. "Gunung Mumbul."

"Good lord," said Gdé Kedampal, who was a well-informed man. He shook his head in wonder. "Just like my Wayan to go after the best … But this is most dangerous. I shall make some inquiries. Now go home. You will speak to no one about this. No one at all, you understand? If this is concluded successfully, you shall be handsomely rewarded. Now off with you."

Dayu Datu was pacing. It was dusk, and Klinyar had not yet come back. At supper the previous evening her place stood empty. The following morning her bed was still undisturbed. Before noon, pieces of her jewelry started to disappear.

On the second evening, Dayu Datu canceled her classes, and the place was stinging with gossip: Klinyar was dead; Klinyar had been banished; Klinyar had stolen the Secret of Secrets (whatever that might be) and fled; she had been kidnapped; she had eloped with Wayan Buyar.

"Well, you know, she might just be lost in some tourist hotel on the beach," said a creamy girl named Selang. She had always felt Klinyar to be her rival.

"Klinyar doesn't get lost," said another girl, generally known to be in love with Klinyar. Her eyes were so swollen from crying that they looked like two pairs of lips.

"Then she must be dead. I'll have her mattress," said Selang. A great hooting and howling went up through the dormitory as the young witches variously mourned their darling or set about looting her belongings.

Dayu Datu listened to this disorder from her office, which she was reconstructing in an exercise to clear her mind. She was installing an elevator, a complicated and exacting chore that she was undertaking for the first time. The noise from the dormitory merely propelled her further upward. But the office itself, when she stepped into it from the elevator, felt wrong: too large, too quiet. She disliked the vast view of the coast; she found the air-conditioning smelly and the paintings inane. She took the elevator back to the ground floor and sent it and the rest of the office to hell.

Now outside, in the middle of her own courtyard, she heard the girls screeching in the dormitory.

"I bet you anything she's pregnant."

"I think she's flunked out."

"Oh, get off it, Selang. She could paint you with your own shit and you wouldn't know it. Klinyar was the best."

"Funny how she could never remember your name. What is your name, anyway?"

"Look — a gold embroidered training bra. And my earrings, the little slut."

"Those are Klinyar's!"

Someone else sang out: "Ni Klinyar, the witchery star. Passed out drunk in a tourist bar."

"If you say her name again I'll kill you!"

And so on. Dayu Datu threw a curse of diarrhea over the whole dormitory and shut them away from her attention. Alone, she walked along the walls of her compound and then flew to the tallest banyan tree on Gunung Mumbul and scanned the sky: "Klinyar, you little harpy, where are you?"

Dayu Datu scanned the landscape of her soul, where Klinyar had resided like a brilliant pet for almost seven years. She saw only mangroves and elevator gears.

And then she knew. The idea stole over her like the paralysis of cyanide: the quarry had made the first strike. But of course. They'd killed Klinyar; it was so obviously the way to disturb her mental equilibrium.

Dayu Datu spontaneously admired the elegance of the gambit; then, having made note of the class of her adversary, she spun off into a horrible howl of anguish.

"Klinyar! Klinyar, my perfect jelly, my kitten, my bundle of diamonds, my pillow, my little aquarium, my Klinyar! Oh, Klinyar!"

Dayu Datu launched herself into the night sky on a scream of curses and grief, causing queer tides, earth tremors, power failures, viruses, landslides, traffic accidents, earaches, fat fires, miscarriages, an inexplicable proliferation of mosquitoes, and the disgorging from the earth of such a variety of stinging and flying ants that simple people everywhere said, "Witches."

All night the air was filled with the stink of burning feathers and violated graves and sounds that made virtuous women cover their ears. Many people died that night, from defeat by long disease, in suicides and freak accidents. Several rivers choked on their own boulders and sent floods over kitchen gardens, orchards, and small holdings of rice fields. Fishes and eels were found dead the next day in treetops; and on the coast, hotels had kept their staff up all night with such emergencies as having to remove, before dawn and without machinery, the corpse of a pony (in harness and with his cart and several abandoned parcels of groceries) floating at the shallow end of the swimming pool.

But this was not yet war.

E<small>VEN ON</small> Gunung Kawi they felt the awful storm. That night the wind was foul and full of the wings of dead insects. Songbirds awoke in the dark and screeched; bees died by the thousands as, disoriented, they crashed in mid-air and stung each other to death. Hell was roaring through the world.

The next day Dukuh Siladri summoned his children and said, "There's a reason for these troubles."

The three of them sat amid the litter of dead songbirds and honeybees, reflecting on the queer violence of the past several days: first, the visit of Wayan Buyar, which so quickly ended in atrocity; next the freakish visitation of Ni Klinyar; and now last night, this hurricane of malevolence.

"It's surely that lout Wayan Buyar who's behind all this," said Mudita.

"Oh yes, I believe so, too," said Siladri. "But that's only the outward circumstance. Why should we be cursed with his attentions in the first place? These strange disturbances are an indication that we've been remiss in some way, and I feel stupid to have overlooked it."

"Overlooked what, Father?" said Kusuma Sari, worried.

Dukuh Siladri gave Kusuma Sari a tender smile. "Your parents, my treasure, have not yet been cremated. It's been over a year. Mudita, you must both go back to Mameling and take care of this. We have been happy here together for too long. It's time for you to assume your duties as head of our family. Your marriage rituals, too, are incomplete. I think it would be wise to see to that as well. You will have to leave without me. You understand that I cannot leave Gunung Kawi, especially now."

Kusuma Sari was startled by the idea of leaving Gunung Kawi. She'd never been farther than the market in the mountain town of Kayuambua.

Siladri read her face. "Don't worry, Sari. Mudita will take good care of you. I suppose Mameling has changed somewhat since we left, but you are formidably well prepared for life, I think. In any case, it is your duty as Mudita's wife to go with him."

"I couldn't bear not to go with him," she said. "But I'll miss you." Kusuma Sari put her arms around Siladri and wept. She longed to tell him that she would always be his daughter, that he was her beloved teacher and protector, the architect of her happiness — for even Mudita had come from him — but all she could say was "Oh, Father" and cry all the harder.

Siladri held and rocked her, wondering why it was that the Dharma was so full of pain. He smiled his anguish at Mudita, whose own eyes were brimming. Finally Kusuma Sari lifted her head and said, "May we come back and visit you?"

"Of course you may," said Siladri, stroking her hair. "But not until these things are done."

They left early the next morning for Mameling, and Mudita was surprised at how quickly the journey went.

All day they walked downhill, through dark groves and dusty villages with sun-baked mud walls. As they descended into warmer country, Kusuma Sari grew excited by the sight of paddy fields. She had never seen wet rice-growing, and she wondered at the ingenious irrigation system that — even in this dry season, when the trees were coated with dust — provided water for trim terraces of emerald-green shoots. As they walked along, Mudita explained to her the rhythms and techniques of the wet rice cycle.

Only half hearing, Kusuma Sari watched him as he spoke; his face was lit with beauty — tender and intelligent. Her lover Mudita swelled, becoming part of this new landscape.

As for Mudita, he felt more protective of his wife with every mile. She had not needed to tell him that she'd renounced sorcery; since her vanquishing of Klinyar, he'd sensed in her a new vulnerability. (They were both reluctant to speak of that magical day, and it would be many years before either of them mentioned it.) Now on the road, Mudita was amused by Kusuma Sari's fascination with the rice fields and wobbling lines of ducks.

"'Dita, tell me. Are there ducks in Mameling?"

"Thousands. It's quite a different world."

They reached the market town of Pujung late in the afternoon.

"Sari, do you know what a *bemo* is?" asked Mudita.

"Those little trucks? Of course I do. I see them all the time at the market in Kayuambua."

"Have you ever ridden in one?"

"No, what for? You know there are no roads on Gunung Kawi. You couldn't get there by *bemo*."

"Would you like a ride in one now? If we take a *bemo*, we can be in Mameling before dark."

"What? Yes, of course. How do you do it?"

Mudita negotiated with the driver of a *bemo* parked near the market, ushered Kusuma Sari into the front seat next to the driver, and climbed in next to her. They felt the little truck bump and sag under the weight of sacks of rice being loaded in the back.

The driver started the engine, and Kusuma Sari, grinning, nudged Mudita. As they pulled out onto the road, she gave a little squeak and laughed and then quickly covered her mouth. Mudita pressed his leg against Kusuma Sari's and winked at her.

Now they were hurtling through the village at thirty miles an hour, and Kusuma Sari's eyes grew wide. With a smile pasted on her face, she watched the world come smashing toward her. Down through the countryside they careered, bouncing and swaying, the houses and fields a flickering blur. Kusuma Sari closed her eyes, but instantly felt dizzy and opened them again. Her smile was starting to sag.

"Just look at the road and pretend you're racing," said Mudita. Kusuma Sari focused her eyes as far ahead as she could, and urged with her heart for the *bemo* to go faster. Suddenly she was grinning again, almost laughing — exhilarated!

As they drew close to Mameling, the traffic grew thick and they slowed enough for Kusuma Sari to see people on bicycles and motorcycles along the road. Coming into the little town, she thought: What big shops! What a lot of lamps! How oddly everyone dresses! At the center of town, the traffic moved at a crawl. It was already dusk, but the market buildings and restaurants were ablaze with light. They passed a very pale man and woman walking by the side of the road, dressed only in what looked like underwear. Kusuma Sari stared and then glanced an unspoken question at Mudita.

"Tourists," he said, smiling at her. "I'll explain later."

It was nightfall when they pulled up in front of the old house compound. Mudita asked the driver to wait a moment, and then they went in through the gate.

Ni Sabuk was sitting at her loom, even though it was too dark to work.

"Ah, Mudita, you're back. It's good to see you." She stretched out her papery hands to him. "And who's this? My word! It's Kusuma Sari. Oh, Kerti was right. This is a special girl. Come here, my little ones, and tell me everything. So you found your father, Mudita. Is he well? And your mother? My little Kadek?"

Mudita looked at his hands.

"Oh no! Oh, poor Mudita. I was worried about her. She was too lovely for this world. Now, Kusuma Sari, you are beautiful, but fortunately you are also intelligent, I see." In fact, Ni Sabuk was now almost totally blind, but no one ever knew it.

Mudita kissed his grandmother, and kissed her again. "Nini, we've come home. But — I'm sorry to bother you with this but, do you have some money for the *bemo* driver?"

The three of them stayed up late into the night, for when Ni Sabuk had finished guessing at their news, she settled back to hear it from them in their own words. She was pleased that they would soon cremate Rajin and Madé Kerti.

"This is right," she said. "It's time to get on with things."

The house was busy for weeks as they prepared for the cremation. The men and women of the village came every day to help make the mountains of offerings that would be required, and the courtyard was loud and gay with voices as people went about their tasks.

Mudita was happy to be at work among his friends again. The men climbed coconut palms to gather young leaves for the women to cut and assemble into offerings; they felled and split bamboo and built light structures to hold the offerings; they slaughtered sacrificial animals and cooked the ritual meats; but the most important work was the construction of a cremation tower and the fabrication of a great-bellied bull in which the corpses would be burned. Mudita himself carved the bull's head from a heavy block of wood.

Kusuma Sari worked with the women and learned much about the goings-on of Mameling. And, of course, she heard many affectionate stories about her parents, and asked many questions. Although people normally tried to be cheerful when preparing for a cremation, the women sometimes wept to think that Kusuma Sari had never known her mother and father, and that they had never had the chance to see what a fine young woman she had become.

When the appointed day drew near, a complex series of rituals began. The souls of Madé Kerti and Rajin were bidden to return from the netherworld and enter a pair of chaste effigies fashioned from magical leaves. These were given daily offerings of food, as if they were living beings. On the morning of the cremation, people arrived at the house with great bundles of firewood. Others brought gifts of raw rice, coffee and sugar, incense, and yards of white cloth.

Outside the gate, a pristine cremation tower rose glittering and white, decorated all around with gilt paper. Next to this stood the black velvet bull, smiling, trimmed in gold braid and garlanded with flowers. The unmarried men of the village waited outside, wearing nothing but a length of black-and-white-checked cloth around their hips: they would carry the heavy platforms of the tower and the bull. A small marching orchestra of cymbals, drums, and gongs waited with them.

Inside, the rest of the villagers sat quietly around the courtyard. As people came in Kusuma Sari greeted each person tenderly, smiling anxiously, for she had never witnessed a cremation. Every villager was served a glass of coffee and a little plate of sweets, as local etiquette demanded. It made no difference to the ladies thus served that they themselves had made the sweets days before. Today, everyone was a guest.

Suddenly the villagers got to their feet and began milling around the east pavilion as Ni Sabuk passed out ritual implements to be carried to the graveyard: baskets of offerings, bottles of holy water, rolled up mats. Some men carried firewood and others carried hoes tied with strips of funerary white cloth. Outside the drum struck three times and the orchestra crashed alive.

Mudita and then Kusuma Sari appeared at the front gate, carrying on their heads the effigies of Rajin and Madé Kerti. Amid the pounding of cymbals and drums, they tucked the effigies into the tower, and the entire company moved off in procession to the cremation ground.

At the graveyard, the villagers crowded around as the corpses of Rajin and Madé Kerti were exhumed — a single mass now, and considerably decomposed. Together with their friends and neighbors, Mudita and Kusuma Sari washed the double corpse and wrapped it in fresh cloth. They bit their lips and Kusuma Sari wept as she poured spring water over her dead mother's hair. Then with long prayers and many gifts (betelnut, tobacco, snapshots), the remains were lifted gently into the bull.

The fire was lit. Mudita and Kusuma Sari, already covered in sweat and grime, stepped back and held each other's hands. Men poured kerosene along a length of bamboo onto the fire. There was a roar, and black smoke and orange flames climbed up the tasseled bull. Smoke poured from the bull's smiling mouth, and in a moment its belly was a glowing, pregnant cage. For an instant, the faces of

Rajin and Madé Kerti were revealed as the flesh burned away and their skulls appeared, face to face in an unending kiss. Kusuma Sari stared, hypnotized, as if witness to her own conception. Love was riding over her on slow smoke. Love and rising, floating bits of ash wafted through her hair, smarted her eyes, and waltzed past her circling slowly upward, leaving a sting in her nostrils. Fire became everything, burned everything. On fire and smoke, the souls of Rajin and Madé Kerti were sent into the sky.

Late in the gray afternoon, Ni Sabuk directed the gathering and combing of the ashes. In a stupor of grief, Mudita and Kusuma Sari furrowed in the warm wastes of the fire, searching for bits of bone incompletely burned. These they collected and ground in a mortar until all that remained of Madé Kerti and his wife was a damp powder. They placed this transcendental chaff inside a young yellow coconut and carried it in swaddling clothes to the sea, the drum-and-cymbal orchestra slashing the way before them.

On the beach, at the edge of the human world, they gave up to the tides all last traces of Rajin and Madé Kerti, and set them afloat to dissolve in the heaven beneath the sea.

Forty-two days later, when the period of mourning was over, Mudita and Kusuma Sari began preparations for their wedding rituals, and again the house was busy. The women of the market circuit talked about the approaching wedding, and so it was that the news reached the neighborhood of Tumbensugih and, eventually, the ears of Wayan Buyar.

Gdé Kedampal was distressed by the slow recovery of his son. Although the wound on his neck was no longer infected, it was healing into an ugly scar that looked like the grimace of a furious monkey. Moreover, Gdé Kedampal could see that his son was very unhappy.

Wayan Buyar stayed in bed for weeks. He responded to his father only with a low growling, although he continued to be articulate with the servants and he bit several of them. With his friend Pegok, who had stayed away as much as possible, he was also lucid.

"So, how're you feeling, Buyar?"

"Eat it."

"Look at you! What a pretty scar. You're going to be uglier than ever."

Wayan Buyar sat up. He was glad to see his friend, but he didn't want to admit it. Instead, he said, "Have you heard anything?"

"About what?"

Buyar slapped Pegok hard across the face. "You nitwit! About our contract."

Pegok stepped back, holding his cheek. "*Your* contract, you mean." A little trickle of blood appeared under his left nostril. "No, I haven't heard anything. Ask your father."

"I beg your pardon?" Wayan Buyar crouched on the cot.

Pegok backed away another step. "You're a turd, Buyar. Your old man's been crying his eyes out for weeks because you won't talk to him — one of your flunkies told me. Why don't you talk to him? He might even be able to tell you how Dayu Datu is doing on your case."

Wayan Buyar thrashed the blankets with his arms and legs. To Pegok he looked like a dung beetle floundering on its back.

"You told him! You oyster-faced traitor! I can't believe my ears!" Suddenly he stopped thrashing and said in a soft, almost musical voice, "Oh, 'Gok. This is all your fault, you know. All, all, all. You're next."

Pegok, staring at Wayan Buyar, wiped his nose on his wrist. He glanced at the blood. "Pity you're not well enough to go to a wedding with me today. Your girlfriend from Gunung Kawi is getting married in Mameling, right under your sticky snout."

Then, with deliberation, he spit on the floor and left.

Ni Sabuk's house was festooned all around with fresh young coconut leaves, and inside, the courtyard was full of wedding guests. The entire village was present, turned out in their brightest clothes. Delicate music from the *angklung* orchestra floated above the walls, and the air was sweet with incense and fresh flowers. The crowd gathered around the bridal couple, who were seated on mats before the east pavilion, where Ni Sabuk assisted the priest.

Mudita wore a rich red cloth brocaded with gold thread which was wrapped around his chest and hung down over his sarong. The family kris was sheathed behind his shoulder. He wore a headcloth of purple brocade and a hibiscus flower behind each ear. Kusuma Sari was dressed in silks of mineral blue and sharp pink. Her long hair hung down her back in a cascade of frangipani blossoms.

At the height of the rituals, Ni Sabuk held up a square of plaited leaves and told Kusuma Sari to hold the other side in her left hand. A merry buzz went through the crowd of wedding guests. This was the moment of symbolic consummation, when the bridegroom pierces the mat with his kris. Mudita smiled at Kusuma Sari and stood up. He took his kris from its sheath. The crowd grew loud and pressed in closer.

"Stick it in good, Mudita!"

"Don't let it get cold, 'Dita!"

Mudita plunged the kris through the mat and the company cheered. Suddenly a half-clad man hurtled into their midst and lunged toward Mudita, trampling offerings, tripping over Kusuma Sari's knees, a roar coming from his bulging neck and purple face.

"You again!" gasped Kusuma Sari.

Wayan Buyar clawed at Mudita, and he rammed his knee into Mudita's groin, knocking the kris from his hand. The villagers jumped up, and the men surged forward as Wayan Buyar grabbed the kris — but before they could pounce on him, Buyar yanked Kusuma Sari by her flowered hair and held her across his chest, the kris just touching her neck. Mudita dived forward. Two men caught him as they would a fish, and two more came to haul him, writhing, to a corner. "'Dita, calm down. We'll take care of this, but we have to keep cool-headed."

Wayan Buyar laughed and adjusted his grip of Kusuma Sari so that his forearm crushed her breast. In a giggly high voice he said, "Don't anyone bother me right now or you'll mess up the bride."

Mudita jackknifed out from under the men restraining him. "Pig! Don't you touch my wife!" They pounced on him again.

"He's upset," murmured Buyar to Kusuma Sari. Then, in a short, quick twist, he sliced off her earlobe.

Everyone froze.

"I told you," Buyar crooned. "I'm busy now." He smiled and showed his awful, wide-spaced teeth. He tossed and tumbled the blood-sticky earlobe and its earring in his hand. His penis stiffened and poked against Kusuma Sari. "There's a ... wedding! ... going on. So please make way for the bride and groom."

Kusuma Sari, staring at nothing, rigid as a plank of wood, was immobile in Wayan Buyar's grip. Only the blood streaming down her neck showed that she was alive. Buyar pushed his feet against hers and turned toward the gate. Mudita lunged forward again, dragging three men with him.

Wayan Buyar turned and tucked Kusuma Sari closer against his body. "The disappointed suitor! Let's give him a little souvenir." He flung Kusuma Sari's earring at Mudita with its little appendage of flesh, and hissed, "The next cut is a tit, then an arm. You'll never touch her alive again, pretty boy."

Mudita reared into the air and was brought down by a pile of his friends. One of them shouted, "Somebody get some holy water!"

The villagers let Wayan Buyar squirm away with Kusuma Sari — but the moment he'd gone out the gate, the men squeezed together in a furor of planning.

"Where's he from?"

"You, go follow him. Bring someone to report back!"

Then an unfamiliar voice spoke up.

"I'll bring you to his house," said Pegok. "Bring your hardware."

Kusuma Sari lay in a heap on Wayan Buyar's cot. "Why aren't you smiling?" he said. Buyar propped her up and then, ignited by her passivity, he hauled her to the floor and leaned her against his wardrobe, the full-length mirror there doubling his pleasure.

"I want you to be smiling. This is the happiest moment of your life! Come now, what's-your-name, let's turn around and smile for B'li Wayan." Wayan Buyar hefted and shoved Kusuma Sari until she was turned full face into the mirror. "You don't look very attentive," he said, and gave her a hearty kick on the back of her head. She keeled over sideways.

In a fury, Wayan Buyar tore the mattress off his cot and hurled it to the floor. The mattress merely sagged silently.

"What's wrong with the world!" cried Wayan Buyar to the stuffy air. He clenched his fists, and his brow plunged down toward his nose. He glanced at the mirror to see how this looked. It wasn't too bad, he thought. At his feet, in a silky crumple, was his prize, a tender rivulet of blood still pulsating from her wound. Wayan Buyar thought this heartbreakingly pretty.

"She loves me the best," he said to his reflection, admiring his body with his hands.

He recomposed himself in the mirror, crouching ferociously, raising his elbows in a classical pose of threat. Terrifying! he thought. He drummed his feet, crouched deeper, raised his elbows higher, and splayed his palms. Magnificent! He curled his left wrist over his breast. My liege, he told himself, here I am, your humble warrior, ready to bite your enemy to bits! He lifted his head in a snicker and bared his teeth to the mirror, then ducked his head and danced quickly in place.

Pegok was crouching outside. "Don't worry," he said to the village headman of Mameling. "He's gone nuts. No problem. Take him out."

WITH EVERY DAY that Klinyar did not return to Gunung Mumbul, Dayu Datu became more distracted. She redecorated her office half a dozen times, trying futilely to create an environment in which she could get into a professional mood. She experimented with a morgue, a Soviet airport lounge, a crack house, an immigration office, an abandoned mine shaft, and a showroom for swimming pool filters — but still she seethed with longing for Klinyar, and her heart was skewered by remorse for having sent her pet along to Gunung Kawi.

She wasn't ready, thought Dayu Datu over and over. I delegated too much. I should have gone myself. That Siladri is obviously a first-class magician. Klinyar was too young. I should have done the research myself. The client even said that Siladri was a witch. But who would have believed that awful creep?

Dayu Datu brooded: Gunung Kawi, that's a venerable address. Dukuh — that meant problems: an ascetic. Her usual opponents were "black" witches like herself — professionals for hire — although none was yet her equal. Occasionally she'd had to deal with some dainty old temple priest; that sort was surprisingly resilient. The artist in her asked, What is the technical advantage these silly old people have? They have no flair, most of them. They are exhaustingly conventional: flowers, starvation, always schmoozing with losers. But there was no doubt that these Dharma dolls, as she privately called them, were tough work. She must remember in the future to charge double for ascetics.

Dukuh Siladri. Gunung Kawi. "Posing as a holy man," the client had said. We'll see.

At last Dayu Datu decided: she would employ classical warfare.

She called her minions together, students and animals. To prepare them for battle, she ordered a feast of undercooked meats, chillies, thistles, and arak. The courtyard filled with smoke from the cooking fires and oil torches, and from the fires of blacksmiths forging weapons.

Some students and animals played noisy music on a mat in a corner, others stripped off their clothes, painted their faces, and danced around with knives and balls of fire. Students mated with animals, instantaneously creating hybrids that danced along with them.

Dayu Datu sat quietly in a small pavilion perched on high stilts and closed off with colored cloth. A little red lamp glowed inside. As the momentum of the evening rumbled toward midnight, the feasting grew louder and more wild, and the silence from Dayu Datu's pavilion grew redder.

Suddenly the curtains of the pavilion began to vibrate, and everything grew quiet. The only sound was a little bell being tapped by a girl with the head of a dog. And then the curtains parted, and the unholy company shuddered.

The creature that appeared was so horrible that the lamps blew out in shock; the only light came from the embers of the cooking fires. The creature held a white cloth over its face, muffling its grunting and chortling, but even in that dim light, all could see the huge hairy hands and long bear-claw fingernails, its huge, swinging whiskery breasts and genitals, and the blue slime of its necklace of entrails. The stench was suffocating.

The monster slowly let the cloth fall away, and the company screamed and scrambled about, ignited by the terrible ugliness of the face. Its huge head was covered in long matted orange fur, and the lips of its snout were curled back by two curving tusks. A great gray tongue disgorged itself and hung down over the monster's belly. And the eyes were huge, red, and insane.

Thus Dayu Datu, incarnated by Durga, the queen of hell, appeared before her troops.

Suddenly she fluttered to the ground and began to move among her minions, muttering filthy oaths and flapping her white cloth. Then she raised her claws high in the air and screamed, "Witches!"

> *Witches! Witches streaming through me!*
> *Stream through me! Eat me! Eat my fire,*
> *Eat my hatred! Take my fire for your magic!*
> *Make murder, make murder, witches!*

A terrible crash of drums broke out, roaring and clashing as the air filled with thousands of creatures: centipedes, stinging reptiles, galloping carcasses, monsters in the guise of razors, old toothbrushes, broken filing cabinets, empty gas bottles, plastic bags of old lasagna, charred airplane parts — all thundering through the air.

Dayu Datu shrieked, "To Gunung Kawi, my babies!"

Siladri woke in the night, sweating and cold. He pulled a blanket around his shoulders and hurried out to the high pasture beyond the gates.

From far away, he could hear the low rumble of the coming attack; then he made out the clattering and screeching and flapping and moaning of the advancing army. A creeping darkness blotted out the stars, and then the hellish storm swung into Gunung Kawi with all the force of an earthquake.

The forest animals began to gallop, and to roar in the old language. The great banyan tree in front of the house split and dropped half of its great size down to the roots, in wood that was instantly dead.

Siladri sat down cross-legged in the pasture and went deep into meditation. Soon a lavender-blue light emanated from the earth, rising, growing taller and brighter, and humming with a most beautiful music.

Dayu Datu's army, boiling and putrid, crashed through the forest of the foothills, spewing tar and infecting the air with radioactivity. Up the mountain they roared, searing the ground as they hurtled toward the summit.

The magical light swelled, incandescent and sonorous, until Gunung Kawi itself was as radiant as a diamond and resonant with the sounds of heaven. Two miles into the sky rose the musical blue light.

As the horde slammed into the holy mist, a freezing catalepsy knocked the hell-shapes useless. The sky above Gunung Kawi was thick with falling devils. They dropped to the ground and lay there jerking helplessly.

And now the forest animals came out. Bright blue, they swooped and cantered gracefully over the ground, back and forth, trampling the fiendish trash until it sputtered and disappeared.

Long after the attack was over, the blue animals gamboled through the light in a carousel of melody.

A small clatter of witches, wheezing and ragged, returned to Gunung Mumbul. Dayu Datu, once again in her natural form but with a few curls of dried entrails sticking to her dress, received the scraps of her army in the kitchen. There was much boohooing on the part of the girls, and furtive insinuations of blame and self-exoneration. Dayu Datu served them a tepid pork soup. As soon as they'd finished eating, she told them to shut up and sent them to bed.

Soon Dayu Datu was alone in the kitchen under a flickering neon light. Absent-mindedly she pinned up her sleepy eyelid with a thumbtack. The kitchen table was sticky and cluttered with dirty plates, and it wobbled slightly. She rested an elbow on the table and lay her cheek in her hand. An old radio sputtered in the background, half-tuned to a pop station in Manila.

Dayu Datu stretched out her other hand and examined it: she thought she might leave her nails long. She looked around at the mess on the table and finally poured herself a glass of arak.

She took some cigarettes from her pocket. The night had not been a success. There was something at Gunung Kawi that was getting in her way, something new, something unknown. But not entirely unfamiliar. She pulled on her cigarette. Unknown: but familiar. The neon light buzzed and blinked. Dayu Datu glared at it with loathing for a moment, and the bulb popped and died.

She sat quietly in the dark. Shards of the fluorescent tube glittered in her hair and floated in her glass, adding an agreeable texture to the arak.

Unknown: but familiar. Slowly tears rose in Dayu Datu's eyes — that bothersome allergy she associated with Klinyar. She mumbled, "Somebody send me Klinyar," but no one came. The room was empty except for Dayu Datu and the dark and the dirty plates and the bottle of arak and the cigarette smoke, which seemed to be trying to escape the room.

Unknown: but familiar. She stared again at her hand and then at her glass. There was something. She knew that — there was always something. Or another. Now there was something about Gunung Kawi, but she couldn't quite think what it was. She poured another glass of arak.

A problem is unknown — but familiar. The outcome is unknown. But when you get to it, it's familiar. Enemies are unknown. "We are not familiar with our enemies," said Dayu Datu out loud, for she was drunk now, "and we do not entertain."

We do not entertain familiarity. *Famil.* We are not famil with our staff. Well, sometimes. We are not famil with our enemies.

Or are we?

"Careless," she said out loud. She swept her arm in a great arc over the table top, pushing the dirty dishes to the floor.

Dayu Datu stood up and swung in place for a moment, and then she walked evenly from the kitchen to her little apartment.

On Gunung Kawi, Siladri too was sitting alone. He had sent the animals to bed after calling them to him, thanking them, and washing their faces in holy water.

He sat in the wide pasture where he and the animals had repelled the attack of Dayu Datu — the same pasture where he had last held his beloved Kadek, and sat with Kusuma Sari when she was still a baby, and felt the eyes of his teacher upon him in the days when he had lost his speech.

Siladri was drawn to this high pasture, most probably, because of its view. Yes, the view, thought Siladri. The view was almost entirely sky.

The night was moonless, but the sky was still incandescent with the evaporating glow of war. Far away to the southwest Siladri could see Gunung Mumbul, a streak of sulfurous glowing. Siladri sat in the high pasture and stared through the night at Gunung Mumbul.

One, thought Siladri: she is a witch of formidable ability.

Two: she is trying to kill us. Or to kill Mudita and me and capture Kusuma Sari for her client — there's no other possible explanation. But she does not know where the children are.

Three: if she kills me, that is of no consequence except to Mudita and Kusuma Sari, and therefore it is of consequence. If she kills Mudita, Kusuma Sari is still in danger. If she kills Kusuma Sari … well, that is not what her client has asked her to do, is it? And if she captures Kusuma Sari, then it is worse than murder, and in any case she would have to kill Mudita and me first.

Four: shall we be forced, then, to kill Dayu Datu?

No.

It's wrong.

And what's wrong with doing wrong?

The consequences — a sin is paid for with one's own suffering.

Well, so what? I have suffered enough from my own spiritual ambitions, and paid so dearly for them with my precious wife, that

I think there is no longer any pain that I'm afraid of. But if I can spare pain to my children by interceding now, then I would be almost happy to suffer again.

So then. I am prepared to commit a sin to protect my children.

I am prepared to kill Dayu Datu.

But if I kill her, then I make my children the children of a murderer. And they would not be free of that for generations.

Now Siladri had a vision: Kusuma Sari wedded to Wayan Buyar in penance for the crime of her father; and Mudita a servant of Wayan Buyar, sharing his sister's penance, hastening the purification of their father's crime by extreme sacrifice. They mustn't know. I cannot commit this crime in my own person, or it would enslave my children — and risk commingling with unsavory blood, too.

So, five: I must kill Dayu Datu in disguise.

And six: thus, I must also use black magic.

Well, so it must be.

And now seven: He made a long and unadorned appeal to all that he could recall of the heavenly in his experience: to Kadek; to Mpu Dibiaja. He called out to them, saying, "You my beloved who are departed from this confusing place that is life-on-earth, please listen! Please listen and tell me, by whatever signs you can send me, what I should do!"

There was no sound, and no sign — nothing but the big night sky and the damp grass beneath him where he sat.

Siladri prayed again, saying "Holy ancestors, holy teacher, perfect mate of mine, show me just the smallest sign that you can hear me!"

Siladri listened and heard nothing but the same sounds of wind in the trees that he had heard ever since he could remember. It occurred to him that perhaps his ancestors, his parents, and his wife had long been set loose from those forms by which he named them.

He simplified his prayers, then, and said through the speech of his heart: In the coming-into-being, in the dissolution-of-being, and in the steadiness-of-change, is there no one who will hear me?

For an hour or more, Siladri listened to the sounds of the night on Gunung Kawi, and he did not dare move a limb, and barely breathed.

Finally he said, but this only to the companion that was his soul: So here we are, then. All is as it appears to be after all. Things are such as they are. I am Siladri, a man getting old. There are things to do, and I must do them without the comfort of heavenly instruction or heavenly promises. God is perhaps concerned with greater things. He doesn't warn me. He doesn't warm me. I would have liked God to speak to me before I die.

A sharp little cramp in Siladri's neck reminded him that only a few hours before he had worked in concert with supernatural forces.

Yes, I know, Siladri thought, but that was work. What I'm about to do — is that in the course of goodness? Or only my private sin?

The scrupulous heart of Siladri could find no answer.

Meanwhile, Dayu Datu stood before the little sink in her bedroom and undressed. There was a mirror above it that she didn't like; it had come with the sink, with a mean, poking little towel rack. Dayu Datu took off her clothes and turned toward the bed, and then turned again toward the sink. She would wash out her clothes.

She had never varied this routine.

She had never before been defeated, however temporarily, but that was no reason not to wash out her clothes.

"Laundry is familiar, and let us at least respect the familiar," she said, but just audibly; she was now very tired. She turned on the tap, and water gushed into the sink, splashing the floor. She wavered over the tap, turned it down, and tossed in a bar of soap.

Well, anyway, it's soap. She turned off the tap and squished her dress into the water. She washed and rinsed it thoroughly, attentive to all the details of private technique, wrung it hard, then spread it over a tree stump outside her house, too tired to enjoy this mild sacrilege.

It was that dark, cold hour of the night that is a hole in time just before morning. Dayu Datu went inside and looked into the mirror over her sink — just a glance — and began to clean her face with tap water. She plucked out the thumbtack in her brow and moved her hands in a circular motion over her face as she had always done, ever since she could remember. She looked at her clean face and examined the new lines that had set around her eyes. She made note of these.

Naked, she turned to her little bed and lay face-down on it, tucking a small pillow under her chest. Now be quiet, she told herself. We will think of Klinyar in the morning.

The tiger and the monkey traveled swiftly to Gunung Mumbul; they did not encounter any swamps. No sooner had they left Gunung Kawi than they were clambering toward the compound of Dayu Datu.

The monkey was lightweight and irritable, and quickly reconnoitered the pavilions; the tiger was heavy and wise, and paced the walls of the compound. The two met in the shadow of the great entry gate. The monkey spoke first.

"She's asleep in that little pavilion over there. Passed out drunk, by the smell of it."

"Try to scare her out over the wall," said the tiger. "I'll take care of her from there. But you must wake her and get her over the wall. Agreed?"

"Agreed."

Bounding along the roofs of the compound, the monkey went back to the quarters of Dayu Datu. There he dropped to the length of his arms and peered in under the eaves at the famous witch, sprawled in the narcosis of sleep.

Dayu Datu lay on her stomach, her arms overhanging either side of the little bed. The monkey was disappointed: he would have liked to see her genitals. In this position she looked like a hairless version of his own children, except for the long black and white tresses that spread over one arm. He noted, and later told his wife, that she was snoring.

The monkey slipped through the bamboo slats that met the roof and slithered down into the room.

It was very easy. He picked up the little kerosene lamp from her bedside, scampered up onto the thatch roof, and sprinkled kerosene and sparks all around him.

The fire smoldered in place for a few moments, perked up, and crept like a low yellow fence across the roof.

Now hissing with impatience, the monkey swung down again into the bedchamber of Dayu Datu: he did not want it said of him that he had burned in her bed the most powerful witch in the world. He jumped up to her pillow and screeched in her ear, as best he could, "Fire! Fire!" and then sprang away into the dark.

Dayu Datu awoke in a seizure of choking. "What an awful night," she said aloud, and then the roof beam crashed before her and burst into flames. Dayu Datu pulled the blanket around her and stumbled to the bathroom window, but as she broke through the glass, her blanket caught fire. By the time she found the wall of the compound she was naked again.

From the dormitory came the shrill whinnying of girls being burned alive, and then there was a soft brilliant explosion. Dayu Datu climbed the compound wall, gulping and coughing on her own curses. She stretched her legs to reach impossible toeholds, swung herself up on menacing briers. Just as she reached the top and saw before her the clean black sea of the forest, her face spreading in a smile of freedom and release, the tiger, gathered and waiting on the other side of the wall, sprang twelve feet into the air and caught Dayu Datu in his jaws. Before the tiger landed, he had snapped her spine.

The woman was dead.

The monkey appeared, scrambling along the top of the palace walls, and dropped neatly beside the corpse of Dayu Datu. With a certain clinical care, the monkey turned her over and edged her into the light coming from the burning dormitory. Her thin lips were nearly closed, and the monkey hesitated for a moment before finally sealing the thin sliver of white between her lids. He could not recompose the ironic arch of her left eyebrow.

Dayu Datu's legs were white and partially arched. The monkey straightened them out, but not without stealing a slinking glance at the witch's sex. To the monkey's horror, it was just like his wife's, and so he began to cover her frantically with leaves.

Then there was a second explosion, and the whole compound bellowed into a thunderhead of fire. Within minutes, there was nothing left of Gunung Mumbul.

While the monkey and the tiger told all this to Dukuh Siladri, their old master said not a word, but watched each of them closely, as though counting the hairs that had been scorched.

Finally, when they had finished reciting every detail, he blessed both monkey and tiger, then blessed them again, and a third time, and said, "My thanks go with you, and my heart, too, which you have carried on this terrible work. I wish you peace now in this world of creatures."

The monkey and the tiger bowed their heads politely. Then they looked at each other and shrugged.

"In any case," said Siladri, "permit me to bid you good night."

It was, in fact, almost dawn, and as the monkey and the tiger watched Siladri walk toward his pavilion, and past his pavilion and out into the garden, morning was rising through the trees.

Epilogue

WAYAN BUYAR was killed by the men of Mameling on Mudita and Kusuma Sari's wedding day. Captained by the gray-faced Pegok and still dressed in their festive clothes, they hauled Wayan Buyar from his bedchamber and dragged him into the street. Gdé Kedampal himself climbed the community alarm tower and beat the hollow log, weeping and shouting, trying to drown out the sound of the lynching in the furious dust below; but when his neighbors arrived, they stood around, torpidly smoking cigarettes, and watched as Wayan Buyar lay near dead on the ground. Someone turned him over so that he lay face-up; then Mudita crouched behind him like a husband assisting a birth and sat him up. Kris in hand for the second time that day, Mudita placed the knife point below Wayan Buyar's right ear.

"Now be off, poor man," Mudita whispered, and he plunged the kris deep into his neck.

One by one, each male householder of Mameling came forward and thrust his kris once into Wayan Buyar's corpse, diffusing the responsibility among them. The neighbors of Gdé Kedampal cleared their throats, spat, stomped out their cigarettes. None protested the murder.

Gdé Kedampal was left broken in spirit. He divided his wealth among his neighbors, and said to them, "You have lost me my son. You might as well have the rest of what is mine — it means nothing to me now." For several weeks he wandered the village, nearly mad and living on scraps, until one day Kusuma Sari took pity and invited him to come dwell in their house, where he lived out the rest of his years.

Mudita and Kusuma Sari had five beautiful children, and lived happily ever after. Ni Sabuk lived to such a venerable age that she taught her great-great-granddaughters to weave.

Klinyar returned to her parents, as she had promised. With the help of the Lord God Shiva, she learned to love them — and, as an expression of the god's pleasure, he initiated her into the art of *wayang kulit*, the sacred shadow-puppet theater, and she became one of Bali's most brilliant priest-puppeteers. She confined her use of magic to the consecration of a particular kind of holy water, used specifically for exorcism.

Dukuh Siladri grieved deeply over his crime.

For three days and three nights the forest animals watched Siladri as he sat motionless in the pasture, alternately soaked by rain and parched by the sun.

On the third night, the ghost of Dayu Datu appeared to him. She wore a blanket and was tapping a palm-leaf book in her hand.

Siladri stared at her, numb. "It's you!" he whispered.

Dayu Datu rolled her eyes.

"So it's not over yet," said Siladri.

"Did you kill Klinyar?"

"No. I believe she's still alive. She was alive and well when she left here."

"Where is she, then?" said Dayu Datu. "I can't find her."

"Kusuma Sari sent her home. She told her to go home to her parents."

"Her *parents?*" Dayu Datu was incredulous. "Dreadful people."

"Kusuma Sari told her to give up witchcraft."

"Indeed? What a remarkable idea." Dayu Datu pulled the blanket closer around her shoulders and said, "May I sit down?"

"Oh, please do, I beg your pardon."

The two of them sat together in the dark meadow. "So she's gone, then," said Dayu Datu.

They were quiet for a moment. "Why have you come?" said Siladri. "I think it's not because you are looking for Klinyar."

A night breeze stirred the grass and rippled Dayu Datu's hair. She turned to him, her gaze freezing Siladri under her cocked eyebrow. "Was it you who killed me?"

He looked fully at the ghost now. "Yes. Is it ... does it hurt very much?"

"Horribly."

Now Siladri bowed his head. "Is there anything I can do to help?"

"Don't be ridiculous."

Siladri thought that no mastery of any magic would ever cure his sense of being ridiculous,

Dayu Datu tossed him the palm-leaf book she was carrying. "Not that you need it, but it belongs here. It belonged to our father."

Siladri stared at the milky apparition. "*Our* father?"

"I've just been with him. Mpu Dibiaja. He sends his love."

"Mpu Dibiaja is our father? You are my sister? What, please, are you talking about?"

Dayu Datu drew up her legs and wrapped them in her blanket. "Mpu Dibiaja was a Brahman priest from Singaraja. You and I were his children — twins. One of his wives hated our mother, and you were given away as a baby to a couple from a distant village."

Ni Sabuk, thought Siladri. Mameling.

Dayu Datu continued. "Ni Sabuk and her husband were students of our father."

"Students?" Siladri felt faint.

"Our father was known as Pedanda Sakti Gdé — a high-powered high priest, obviously. And, well, you know how it is with clever priests. There were always people coming around with broken arms and mad sisters, always people wanting to borrow books ... There were followers, if you see what I mean."

"He was already, well, wise?"

"He was already a witch, yes. And then something awful happened to the other wife, and he left and became Mpu Dibiaja."

Siladri's ears were ringing in amazement. "Do you remember this? Do you remember him?"

Dayu Datu stared out across the field and across the sky to where Gunung Mumbul had been. "I remember our mother, and our father, and the other wife. I remember everything. Our mother was very beautiful. And very weak. She was younger than this other wife, who was an ugly thing with an ugly little boy — she was jealous of us. She had stolen a book from our father and was using it to kill our mother. So I used it to kill the other wife first. Not that it helped anything. I have seen our mother, too. She looks terrible."

"Is she with ... our father?"

"It's not like that."

Siladri felt a storm of grief building in his heart. He tried to blink away his confusion. "What's this you say about killing with books?"

"Well, you know, I was only a little girl, about the age of Klinyar when she first came to me. I didn't know anything, really, except that I saw that woman steal a book — small people in big houses see a lot — and that the more she studied the book, the sicker our mother became." The ghost's face grew long and angular. "She could become lost in her own room. She used to think I was you."

Siladri felt as though he had turned to ice.

"So one night I went to the other wife's room. She was crouched like a vulture over her reading table, moaning her dirty spells. She didn't see me. There were two books on the table, one open in front of her, the other one closed, and a black-and-white-checked cloth on the mat beside her."

Siladri nodded. "The books' wrapping."

"Mmm. Anyway, there she was. I didn't even have to think. I grabbed her from behind and rammed the book she was reading down her throat. Filthy sow. When she was finally dead, I pulled the book out, put it in my shirt, and stuck the other one in her throat."

"My word," mumbled Siladri. "And then?"

"Then I took the weapon book —"

"The weapon book?"

"*That* book, the one in your hands!"

"I'm sorry. Do go on."

"I took the book and went to live on the south coast. I knew that people there wouldn't pay much attention to where I'd come from."

"How did you know that?"

"I'd heard. Anyway, I found work there. Not very nice work, but never mind. And I studied — that book. And whatever else I could learn. Eventually I didn't need to work for other people anymore, only clients."

"I see," said Siladri. "Poor girl."

"Oh, don't cry. I hate that," said Dayu Datu. "I did very well."

"So I understand, in a way. For a while ..."

"And then you killed me, and here we are."

Again they were silent. Finally Siladri said, "You know this is all very extraordinary."

"Yes," said Dayu Datu.

"Forgive me if I trouble you with such a question, but I must ask it. How do things stand between us now?"

Dayu Datu smiled at him from beneath her ironic brow. "Do you mean, shall I exact my revenge?"

"Well, yes."

"No. I have come to thank you."

"Thank me?"

"You are most repetitive, Siladri. I wonder how your wife could bear it. Yes, I want to thank you for having put an end to that awful life of mine, for having stopped me from committing any more of those tiresome crimes."

Siladri looked at his sister. She did indeed look very much like him. The night sky was fading; the field around them began to evaporate, disappearing into itself in a play of indistinguishable grays; dew collected in their hair. The apparition of Dayu Datu began to waver. Siladri stared hard at his renegade twin — trying across death, to memorize her features. She was grisly and beautiful at once, like his own soul.

"So, then," he said, "do you forgive me?"

"I forgive you. Let us wish each other peace."

Dukuh Siladri still lives on Gunung Kawi. He no longer grows old, and is invisible to all but the pure in heart; but the honey from Gunung Kawi is abundant, sweeter and more wonderful than ever, and free for anyone who can find it.

Acknowledgments (1992 edition)

I am grateful to I Gusti Madé Sumung, Mangku Gdé Padang Kerta, I Madé Sija, I Madé Pasak Tempo, and A. A. Alit Ardi for helping to reveal to me the beauty of the tale "Dukuh Siladri".

I am grateful to Wendy Whiteley, Cody and Lyn Shwaiko, Roxana Waterson and Garth Sheldon, Bill Milberger, Alfred Barrett, Dennis Robinson, Howard Hertz, and Tucker Viemeister for their patient hospitality during the writing of this book, and to Miss Jessie Teng for her gracious help. I am grateful to Chris Carlisle, Roxana Waterson, Bill Milberger, Lansing Pugh, Bob Skolski, Dakota Jackson, RoseLee Goldberg, Sarah Verdone, Edward Behr, Deborah Dunn and Jean-François Guermonprez for reading the work in progress.

I am especially grateful to Laura Gross for representing my work, and to Camille Hykes, my editor, for her nourishing support and guidance. I am grateful, too, to Larry Cooper for his fine manuscript editing.

Notes to this edition

There are several important omissions to the Acknowledgments in the 1992 edition. I am especially grateful to John Darling and Madé Wijaya, who both introduced me to Bali and its enchantment when I first came to the island in 1980. It was in John's library that I first discovered a synopsis of the tale "Dukuh Siladri" and it was with him that I collected oral versions of the story from elderly Balinese friends.

The late Barbara Loveric found me a copy of the entire poem "Dukuh Siladri" in Balinese (Latin script), at the University of Sydney.

And I must add the name of Didier Millet to this list, for offering to publish the book in the first crop of electronic publications by Editions Didier Millet and publishing this latest print edition.

In the course of preparing this edition, it was impossible not to make corrections to spelling and other errors. Neither could I resist cleaning up some of the worst infelicities (such as "a male rooster") and making some very slight revisions, which I hope make it read better.

About the Author

Diana Darling has lived in Bali since 1980. She is married to A. A. Alit Ardi of Ubud.

Rimbaud in Java: The Lost Voyage
Jamie James

128 pp
190 x 133 mm paperback
ISBN: 978-981-4260-82-4

In the first book devoted to Arthur Rimbaud's lost voyage to Asia, novelist and critic Jamie James reviews everything that is known about the journey; from there he imaginatively reconstructs what the poet must have seen and what he might have done, vividly recreating life in 19th-century Java along the way. *Rimbaud in Java* concludes with an inquiry into what the Orient represented in the poet's imagination. James' intriguing book is a rich blend of biography, criticism and thought-travel, bringing into sharp focus this brief encounter between a great writer and a vanished world.

EXCERPT

"The search for points of correspondence between Rimbaud as we know him, the places he visited in central Java, and the year 1876 is like trying to graph a problem in algebra with too many variables. The only solution is to assign values to them imaginatively, which reveals more about the algebraist than the problem. From a modern perspective, the first impulse is to extrapolate from Rimbaud's past, to send him out on a sultry night in Salatiga to get high at the Chinese opium den in the market, to prowl the crossroads looking for sex, like the modern student. It is the perennial temptation with Rimbaud to make him into what one would have him be, like a mother who dresses her child to please herself.

If the first generation of Rimbaud memorializers envisioned him as a doomed seraph too pure for the grossness of this world, a tragic child genius in the mould of Chatterton, the generation born after the Second World War is under the influence of twentieth-century rebels such as Henry Miller, Jim Morrison, Patti Smith and Richard Hell (in a fine novel called *Godlike*), who shaped the image of Rimbaud the outlaw.

Rimbaud in 1876 was undergoing or had recently accomplished a personal revolution. The grimly determined trader and explorer in Africa is a completely different person from the intellectually brilliant adolescent who was always drunk and stoned, and used his dishy good looks and presumable talent for sex to get what he wanted from his elders. The adult Rimbaud lives for us mainly in his letters home, which often reveal an intense homesickness and a sentimental love for his mother and sister that are utterly foreign to the delirious child bacchant of the Boul'Mich.

Solving the problem might begin with the triad of traditional soldiers' pursuits in the tropics and everywhere: gambling, drinking and whoring. The first may be eliminated, for no evidence exists that Rimbaud ever played games of any kind, much less games of chance."

Twilight in Djakarta
Mochtar Lubis

232 pp
195 x 130 mm paperback
ISBN: 978-981-4260-65-7

Mochtar Lubis, in this vivid dissection of social and political life in Jakarta at the beginning of the 1960s, reveals the dark currents of poverty, corruption and vice which course beneath the surface of one of the great cities of the Third World. Although set in Indonesia, the tale that unfolds has universal application as it describes the forces which determine the lives of rich and poor, politicians and criminals, intellectuals and simple rural immigrants alike, as they struggle for survival. Through the character of the central figure, Suryono, a young, Western-educated government official, the author depicts the complex web of threads which enmesh both individual and society in a newly developing nation, with compassion as well as insight.

EXCERPT

"An old delman carriage, empty, drawn by an old emaciated horse, and its driver, Pak Idjo, dozing in his seat, came by, passing in front of the restaurant. For years the horse had been accustomed to pulling the delman through the big city, and even if the driver fell asleep, which often happened on hot days – and Pak Idjo hadn't had any passengers since morning, until he dozed off hungry – the horse continued drawing the delman by himself, stopped by himself when hailed by a passenger, awakening the driver by the shock of the sudden stop. Or when a traffic policeman barred the traffic's progress, the old horse stopped too, its muzzle pressed against the side of a car or a truck.

In this way the horse which pulled the delman cart trotted on along the street also on that gay evening. Near the restaurant, from behind the fence of the house across the street, a big dog chasing a cat suddenly jumped out, barking loudly. The horse, badly startled, tried to dodge the dog and the cat at its feet, slipped and fell; the left pole of the delman with its blackened copper capping hit the side of the red Cadillac at the roadside, damaging its chromium and paint, and the protruding iron brace of the cart roof struck the car's side window, shattering the glass.

Pak Idjo, jolted from his nap, staggered out, helped the old horse to its feet and just stood there, dazed, stroking the horse's knees and head.

The noise of the collision also alarmed the guests who sat eating, drinking and laughing in the restaurant. Raden Kaslan jumped up and hurried to the street; the moment he saw the damaged chromium and paint on his car, and the shattered glass of the door, he flew into a rage."

My Journey from Paris to Java
Honoré de Balzac

64 pp
203 x 135 mm paperback
ISBN: 978-981-4260-14-5

My Journey from Paris to Java is a short fantasy diversion to the mystical island of Java, where Balzac, or rather the *narrateur*, encounters a deadly poison-breathing tree, civilised monkeys, a love-sick sparrow and that epitome of Oriental desirability of his day – the women of Java. Written just before he started on the multi-volume *La Comédie humaine*, this charmingly small work was nevertheless much loved by Balzac and provides a breathtaking view of his imagination.

EXCERPT

"With your permission I will eschew the foolish personal stories with which my predecessors have started their tales. To get to the point, project yourselves at once across the ocean and the Asian seas, traverse the great spaces on a good sailing brig, and let us come at once to Java, my island of choice. If you like it, if my observations are of interest, you will have been spared all the boredom of the journey.

Nonetheless, if you're like me, I pity you. I confess, to my shame, the things that beguile me the most in such tales are precisely those that I understand the least.

When a traveller talks to me of emerging from I don't know which islands, of monsoons, currents, the number of fathoms of water found at a place which I worry about as if they were the bones of Adam, of reefs, records, lochs, high and low gallants, boat tackle, of bolt ropes, sideslips, the state of the sky etc., of flowers and plants ending in *-ia*, of the class of dicotyledons or dichotomons, orobranchoids, with fingers, etc., or of nudibranchs [a kind of mollusc], or clavipalped tentacles, globular horns, marsupials, hymenoptera, dipteroids, bi-valves, no-valves (how do they manage?) etc. – then I open my eyes wide and try to grasp something out of this deluge of barbaric words. Like people who stop on the Pont-Neuf to look down to the river at nothing in particular, seeing everyone else doing the same thing – I am searching for the unknown in the void with all the passion of the chemist seeking to make diamonds by compressing carbonised wood. Such books fascinate me in the same way as staring into an abyss. Reading an incomprehensible work such as *The Apocalypse* – and there are many apocalyptic books in modern literature, above all accounts of scientific travels – is like a game of skittles in the darkness for my soul, like Jacob's struggle with the angel of the Lord. And often it is no more permitted for me to see the angel than it was for the patriarch."

Ring of Fire: An Indonesian Odyssey
Lawrence Blair with Lorne Blair

248 pp
215 x 150 mm paperback
ISBN: 978-981-4260-10-7

The true story behind the award-winning PBS television series, *Ring of Fire* charts the Blair brothers' 10-year sojourn through the world's largest and least-known archipelago – the islands of Indonesia. Amid impenetrable rain forests, erupting volcanoes and startling natural beauty, the brothers have captured on film and in words the story of one of the most captivating and intriguing explorations ever made.

EXCERPT

"The word 'Asmat' means 'Tree' or 'Wood' people, for they are the same word and, like their totemic creature the praying mantis, they are the forest itself come alive. Legend tells how their creator, Fumeripits, carved their first ancestors from trees which he then drummed into life, standing back to watch them dance.

The Asmat also carve trees into which they drum the spirits of relatives killed in battle with neighbouring villages. These spirits can only be released through a vengeance killing. The carving of these spectacular 20-foot bis poles is part of an elaborate ritual which ultimately requires the killing, beheading and eating of at least one retaliatory victim from the offending village or clan. 'Inhabited' bis poles may stand in a village for weeks or even years until anointed with the victim's blood which then releases their residents to eternal rest in the land of ancestors, so the poles can be discarded to rot. More than mere carvings, inhabited bis poles are 'living beings' about whom the entire Asmat religious ecology of revenge and regeneration revolves, but to museums and collectors around the world they rank amongst the most valuable and coveted examples of contemporary primitive art.

Nowadays it is rare enough either to be a bona-fide headhunter or a cannibal, but to be both simultaneously is – at least to a snooping anthropologist – a singular accomplishment. The Asmat were to achieve world fame in 1961 when Michael Rockefeller, son of the late American Vice-President, disappeared off their coast. He was last seen swimming strongly for shore from his drifting open boat towards the nearby village of Otjanep.

Michael Rockefeller was a child of the Steel Age: heir to the most powerful clan of his nation, which had risen on the tide of oil and US Steel. He studied ethnology at Yale and in 1961, aged 22, made his first trip to Indonesian New Guinea (now called Irian Jaya) on a collecting expedition sponsored by the New York Museum of Primitive Art. A few months later he made his second – and last – trip to expand what was already the world's finest single collection of Asmat art (now at the Metropolitan Museum of Art in New York)."